# APACHE C

Angered cattlemen manage to purchase several Gatling guns from unprincipled thieves for the purpose of wiping out the Indians residing in Apache Canyon.

Becoming suspicious, scouts from Fort Winfield Scott trail the wagons and are captured, but as the guns are being delivered to the stockmen's town of Burnt Timbers, the army unexpectedly arrives.

The difficulties are compounded by the discovery of Apaches during the army's pursuit of the renegade cowmen. When the ultimate showdown appears imminent, the Indians prudently withdraw leaving a settlement to be reached between the rival factions of white men – the army and the renegades. The life of Al Whitten, the competent army scout, is threatened in the bloody shootout that ensues, but will the army succeed in its perilous struggle to overcome the cattlemen and free the endangered scouts?

'The best in the business'                    *Kirkus Reviews*

# APACHE CANYON

## HARRY FOSTER

A Black Horse Western

ROBERT HALE · LONDON

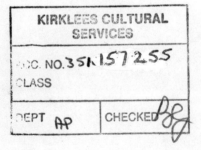

Photoset in North Wales by
Derek Doyle & Associates, Mold, Clwyd.
Printed in Great Britain by
St Edmundsbury Press Ltd., Bury St Edmunds, Suffolk.
Bound by WBC Bookbinders Ltd, Bridgend, Glamorgan.

# ONE
# Men, Horses and Land

New Mexico Territory reached from the westernmost boundary of Texas to the southeasternmost border of California. Not until the second decade of the present century would that Territory be divided into two states, New Mexico and Arizona.

It was the raiding fief of warlike tribesmen of which the most notable, and mobile, were the Apaches, a term originally applied by the Zunis to the Navajo and meant simply 'an enemy'.

The distinction of parts of the Territory were of little importance to the tribesmen. True, those residing in what was to become Arizona had to ride for days in order to raid into what remained New Mexico, but those mobile raiders and accomplished horsethieves raided as they went, so distance amounted to little more than an extension of a time-hallowed custom.

Apache Canyon was somewhere in the vicinity where the ultimate boundary between Arizona and New Mexico would be established in an area running in roughly three directions of *Señora Satán's* hodgepodge of towering rocks, jumbles of indiscriminately scattered boulders, of graceful little paloverde trees, cactus, rattlesnakes, Gila monsters, hairy dark spiders as large as a man's hand, ants that stung like fire, precious little grass and water, creosote and thornpin underbrush and Indians.

No one really wanted that land, especially Apache Canyon which was not very deep and not exceptionally wide, but which meandered for almost three miles like a wound across the belly of an otherwise fairly predictable terrain, and was said to have historically hidden the worst or best, – depending on the colour of the appraiser's hide – marauders in the world.

In springtime the desert country is second to none in the fragrance of its flowers, the purity of its air, the flawlessness of its vistas, and its bunchgrass, the same rich natural source of nourishment called 'buffalo grass' farther north. It sprouts in stools, grows stirrup-high and even when it cures in summer heat, its seedheads still provide strength domestic grasses never achieve.

Animals live off the bunch grass during the early and late spring, after it cures, animals and Apaches both live off the seedheads.

Apaches had the better of it; they could eat what many animals could not, and would not, eat. Horseflesh, rabbits, snakes, lizards, grassheads, bean pods from desert trees – one of which was *peyote*, whose buttons produced hallucinations which were especially significant for second-sight and religious rituals.

Cattlemen had begun encroaching in the south desert a generation earlier. Only when the cattle began appearing in great numbers in springtime cropping bunch grass within something like eight or ten miles of Apache Canyon, did the tribesmen, whose normal practice was to ride and raid over great distances, decide to retaliate for what they perceived as trespass on hallowed ground.

A stocky man sitting on a slightly pigeon-toed, short-backed bay horse in dawn shadows spoke quietly to the tall, leaner man beside him on the tall chestnut wearing a regulation army saddle.

'It's been a long time since any white-eyes got this close to the rim of their canyon.'

The tall, solemn-looking man was watching smoke blossom among the brush shelters concealed among the trees and underbrush below and said nothing. The hairs on the back of his neck had been standing up for three hours. They were still standing up.

The stocky man leaned on the saucer-sized horn of his saddle, also watching belated activity down below. 'What I never been able to understand is why Apaches, of all people, made their village down there.' He got no comment so he shrugged. 'Tradition, heritage; their kinsmen been living down there since gawd knows when.' The stocky man gestured. 'Should have watchers up here. Hell, if we was a regiment of cavalry wouldn't a damned one of them get up out of there alive.'

The tall man was bronzed from exposure, had a slit of a mouth, a slightly hawkish cast to his profile, and was in theory anyway, the superior officer of the stocky man, whose name was Alan Whitten. They both belonged to the company of scouts stationed at Fort Winfield Scott. The tall man was Captain Herbert Morris. His grandfather had come to the New World bearing the name of Fitzmaurice. The captain's father had made things easier for the two-thirds of illiterate Americans who had never pronounced the name Fitzmaurice properly and could not have spelled it if their lives had depended upon it even when they could write and knew the alphabet.

Captain Morris had a rare quality, having come up through the ranks, he had never lost he ability to be easy with other men, especially those under him. He dryly observed that eventually someone was going to ride up out of that canyon, to which Alan Whitten said, 'Yep. An' we'll leave tracks.'

He was correct, but by the time they saw saddle-pad horsemen coursing over their back trail they were close enough to the palisaded log fort not to worry.

The breakfast fires were smoking inside the compound, life at Fort Winfield Scott was bracing for another day, and as Alan Whitten corraled and fed his horse, Captain Morris was reporting his interesting ride with the scout to an open-mouthed major, the post commandant who, when Morris had finished, got red in the face and demanded to know what kind of damned fools would ride up to the edge of Apache Canyon in daylight, to which the captain replied that it hadn't been his intention; he relied on the experience and judgment of his scout.

Major Burroughs sat down, stared, and said. 'The judgment of a damned scout? Captain, you're goin' to get yourself killed. Alan Whitten? Was he sober, for chrissake?'

Morris's lips flattened slightly. 'It was daybreak, sir.'

The senior officer blew out a ragged breath, eyed Captain Morris briefly then gestured toward the door. 'You've reported.'

Captain Morris nodded to the orderly in the adjoining room on his way out.

In the yard men were heading for the wash-house, others were sitting in springtime warmth cleaning weapons, smoking and waiting for the muster of one of the two scouting detachments which fanned out from Fort Winfield Scott each day, usually after an earlier reconnoitre by the post's scouts.

Captain Morris went to his hutment to shave. He had ridden out with Whitten close to midnight for no particular reason except to feel free of army confinement, which he liked to do occasionally. But he had not expected Whitten to stalk right up until they could look down into Apache Canyon. He hadn't felt good about it last night and still did not feel good about it.

There were three civilian scouts at the post. Whitten, a seasoned frontiersman of about forty, was thought to be the wisest, and canniest of the three. Captain Morris had ridden with him before, on routine scouts, they had exchanged ideas, even philosophies and Morris had found Whitten to be compatible, genial, a man with humour who was also very observant and shrewd. That damned trip to the edge of Apache Canyon shook his faith in Alan Whitten. It had been a suicidal stunt for no apparent reason, something Captain Morris had not expected from the scout.

That ragheads had found those shod-horse tracks on the rim above their canyon, and had followed them to within sight of the post, troubled Captain Morris a lot less than the certainty that what he and Whitten had done, had been the equivalent of kicking a hornet's nest.

In wintertime Indian troubles were minimal. In springtime it required very little to agitate them, a condition that commonly prevailed throughout the summer and into the autumn. What he and Alan Whitten had done would have consequences. He was sure of that, and evidently so was Major Burroughs.

It was one thing to scout-up ragheads for a reason, and it was something altogether different to risk one's neck for no reason.

When they met again later, after the first scouting detail had left, Whitten said, 'Wagons east about a day's ride,' and the officer faintly frowned about that. This was the first he had heard of wagons entering their territory.

He went over to the command hutment and asked the orderly about oncoming wagons. The orderly shook his head, he had heard of no such a thing, but the moment Captain Morris departed the orderly went to Major Burroughs with the tale, and the post commander glared. 'How would a damned scout know before we do?'

The orderly returned to his desk wondering the same thing, and late the same afternoon a post-rider arrived who verified that wagons were indeed heading toward Fort Winfield Scott.

The orderly took that information to the major and

Burroughs sat staring at him, both men puzzling over the same thing.

The only lieutenant on the post, Eric Sorenson, a large, rawboned fair man, appeared at the doorway of Captain Morris's hutment to verify a rumour of wagons. Morris acknowledged that wagons were coming, and Sorenson asked a natural question.

'Whose wagons?'

Morris made a tough little humourless smile when he replied. 'Ask Al Whitten. I have no idea whose wagons they are.'

Lieutenant Sorenson, like most frontier soldiers, had come up through the ranks. When he found Alan Whitten leaning on a corral behind his cabin where he kept two horses, he asked about the wagons and Al Whitten smiled. 'Smoke, Lieutenant. I smelled it last night when I was out with the captain.'

'It could have been a grass fire, or In'ians, Al.'

'Could have been for a fact, but it wasn't. Indians don't fry bacon, an' you don't smell grass fires before you see them.'

'Any idea whose wagons they are?'

'No, but judging from the smell I'd say there was a number of them.'

Sorenson went to the major's orderly for more information and discovered that neither the orderly nor the commanding officer knew even as much as he did, so he crossed the compound and told Captain Morris what the scout had said. Morris shook his head. 'He never mentioned a damned thing about smoke last night. But he scairt hell out of me going to the rim of Apache Canyon.'

After the lieutenant departed, Captain Morris went over to the small area allocated scouts, found Whitten bathing in mid-day heat at the creek that ran across the northeasterly part of the compound, and sat down on a rock as he mentioned bacon-scented smoke. Whitten ducked to rinse off and came out of the creek to put on his trousers and fringeless buckskin shirt, with the creases and stains of much use and many cooking fires.

When the officer said, 'Did that scent have anything to do with us riding to the rim of the In'ian's canyon?' Alan Whitten smiled at him. 'I wondered if the ragheads had scouted up the wagons. If they had there would have been horse-activity down there, and there wasn't ... But it might not be a bad idea to send a detachment to escort those wagons. Sooner or later the In'ians will find them.'

Captain Morris sat on his rock contemplating the swiftly flowing water for a long time. 'Do you ever wonder when this mutual hostility will end so folks can get about making farms and ranches out here?' he asked.

Whitten's reply was practical. 'When that happens I'll be out of work. By the time it ends we'll both be a hell of a lot older than we are now ... Did the major send out an escort?'

'Not that I know of,' replied the captain, arising from his rock. 'He didn't know there were wagons out there. By now he does; Lieutenant Sorsenson told his orderly.'

Alan Whitten leaned against one of the posts of his pole corral. When the officer gave it as his opinion that it might be settlers, Whitten refrained from stating his own thoughts that it was more likely a freight train. Spring rains would compel most settler trains to fort up in some town until the ground was hard again. Freighters took mud in stride; they weren't wanderers, they were men of commerce whose profit only accrued when they delivered their loads.

Captain Whitten strolled thoughtfully to the command hutment, met Major Burroughs on the way out with his gauntlets tucked under his belt, and did not have a chance to speak. The heavy-set senior officer with grey at the temples and nine years of frontier service, spoke first.

'The morning detail went west and north. They'd be

out of reach of wagons comin' from the east. Might be a good idea for you to take a detail and scout up those damned wagons.'

Major Burroughs had an aversion to settler trains of wagons. They usually reached the fort with scarecrow livestock, little food and only the most general idea of where they were.

He was tugging on his gauntlets and glancing around the sunbright compound when he also said, 'When you get back let me know,' and went down off the small porch to the compound heading for the horse corrals.

Captain Morris crossed to his cabin, buckled his sidearm into place, left the saber where it was hanging on a peg, and returned to the area of the compound reserved for scouts and their animals.

Alan Whitten was sitting inside with the door wide open eating what looked like cold venison, which he washed down with cold creek water. He looked up when the officer appeared in his doorway and gestured towards a chair at the table. 'Eat up, Captain. We might not get another chance for a long while.'

Morris sat down, eyed the haunch of meat and filled a cup with coffee. 'We're supposed to scout up those wagons.'

Whitten went on eating. 'Interesting thing about the army; by the time something sifts through its routine, a man's had time to fill up before he has to ride.'

Captain Morris was not without humour, but this statement did not amuse him. 'This coffee would float horseshoes,' he said, scowling into the half-empty cup.

Al Whitten smiled. 'I've thought about catching a squaw, but I've seen enough men who did that to pretty well convince me that strong coffee's the lesser of two evils. Are we going alone or with a detail?'

'With a detail. If the major had known before the morning patrol left, he could have sent them east.'

Whitten arose to clear his table and get his shellbelt

and sidearm. 'I'll be waiting when you form up your detail. Meet you at the gate.'

Before leaving, while standing in the doorway. Captain Morris said, 'You smelled bacon frying? Can you smell gold?'

They both laughed. After the officer's departure Al Whitten had plenty of time so he sat down to take care of a chore he'd been putting off; he cleaned and oiled his Winchester saddle gun. He also had a chew of molasses-cured tobacco, and before going out back to rig his horse, he had a pull on a jug he kept secreted behind the iron stove.

It was a beautiful day, as clear and sparkling as days usually were after rain. There was a hint of a little breeze coming off the northward mountains. If a man had hawklike eyesight he could discern a skiff of snow atop the far rims. Winter rarely gave way to springtime with good grace.

The other two scouts, both 'breeds, one much lighter than the other, had been out with a wood-cutting detail for two days and probably would not return to the fort with their wagonloads until evening.

Captain Morris was down at the corrals saddling up with his detail of ten enlisted men. By the time Alan Whitten led his horse over to the massive log gates to pass the time with the sentry Captain Morris had his men mounted and moving.

As they left the fort that little chilly breeze brisked up. The sun was warm enough, it just was not close enough to the earth to offset that cold breeze.

The horses were up in their bits. Because a rotation system prevailed under Major Burroughs, no horse was ridden more than every other day, except for emergencies, then they might all be ridden, depending upon the nature of the emergency.

There were sixty men at the post. Normally that interpreted to forty or forty-five effectives, especially this time of year when men had fever colds, the flux and other ailments.

# TWO
# The Missing Scouts

East of Fort Winfield Scott were whatever vestiges of civilised existence could be found in several towns and a number of villages, the land was better; with trees, grass and water. Indian raids over there had been fairly well eliminated except for the occasional strongheart who had to prove he was worthy by sneaking close, sometimes in broad daylight which was particularly admired among fellow tribesmen, and steal a horse.

Troopers from the fort were too many miles west and south for Saturday night visits to the waterholes of those towns. They existed in a private world for the most part cut off from news unless a post rider happened along, and that only occurred when the more easterly posts, camps or stations thought something worthwhile, like general orders from back east, should be transmitted to outlying, isolated posts.

As Captain Morris rode up ahead of his detail with Alan Whitten he dryly commented on the isolation to which he had become resignedly accustomed, and the scout's reply had been as candid, and at times as impertinent, as frankness required. 'You chose your career.'

A West Pointer would have got red in the face. Captain Morris simply said, 'Yup, I sure did, but it would be nice if they'd rotate us now and then.'

It was mostly open country; there was little danger of
being ambushed, but such was the reputation of the
ragheads that soldiers, even in strong numbers on
patrol, sprouted eyes in the back of their heads.

Two miles east of the fort they had their first sighting
of wagons. Because they were travelling one behind the
other it was a while before the detail could verify that
there were six heavy rigs, obviously riding low and
moving slowly.

Captain Morris halted the detail. They watched two
horsemen come around from the far side of the lead
wagon and lope toward them. Captain Morris frowned.
Six supply waggons in train were unusual. The
customary number was ten or twelve with hired
outriders. This train of six laden wagons seemed to have
only those two scouts heading for the detachment. He
spoke to Alan Whitten without taking his eyes off the
slowmoving freighters. 'If it's re-supplies for the fort,
they must have enough provisions to last until next
year.'

'Or part for us and part for somewhere else,' replied
the scout.

A grizzled, red-faced and redheaded sergeant spoke
gruffly from behind the officer. 'That there feller in the
smoke-tans is Charley Skinner.'

Not another word was said as the oncoming horsemen
closed the rather considerable distance until Al Whitten
confirmed what the sergeant had said. 'It sure as hell is.
I figured they'd have hung him by now.'

The captain said nothing until the outriders slackened
to a steady walk for the last three hundred feet. One of
them looked like a Mexican or possibly a 'breed Indian.
But the man who held the detail's attention was a
thick-shouldered, clearly physically very powerful man
of indeterminate age except for pigeon wings of grey at
the temples. He was weathered to a perpetual bronzed
look, lined, with sunk-set grey eyes and a lipless mouth

like a bear trap that curled faintly upwards at its outer corners.

He rode straight and carried his head high in a challenging manner. As he came close and stopped he smiled at Captain Morris, a very self-assured individual who seemed not to have ever heard the term 'deference' toward army officers or, for that matter, anyone else.

' 'Morning, Captain. We got some supplies for Fort Scott.'

Morris nodded. 'We can use them, Mister Skinner.'

The burly man nodded about that before also saying, 'This here isn't the usual army convoy. The head In'ian just agreed to haul your two wagonloads at the last minute. We're goin' farther west to a settlement called Burnt Timbers. Supplies an' trade goods.'

Captain Morris had been to the Burnt Timbers settlement once, his first year at his present station. At that time it had been a scattering of log structures in the middle of miles of open grassland country. The settlers had been Missouri farmers with a few stockmen. The reason he had gone there that time had been because a particularly savage Indian raid had almost wiped the place out. Evidently it had recovered. He asked the outrider if he'd been out there lately and Skinner nodded. 'A few times. After it was nearly wiped out a while back. Texas drovers come along and now it's a fair-sized place with cattle and ranches.' Skinner smiled. 'Them boys figured the best way to stop trouble was to strike first; they killed In'ians in all directions like most folks kill varmints. It worked; last time I was over there hadn't been a raghead sighted in a long time.'

A large bearded man atop the foremost wagon had a voice like a bull alligator. 'You fellers goin' to set an' talk all day?' he bellowed, and Charley Skinner grinned at Alan Whitten. 'He's an old hand at freighting but he's new out here. We might as well get along anyway.'

The outriders rode back to the halted train, Captain

Morris reversed his course and started back toward the fort. He was silent for a long time. Al Whitten looked back at that red-headed sergeant and winked. The sergeant winked back.

Eventually Captain Morris said, 'That's the Charley Skinner there's so many legends about? Seemed to me to be like any other hired outrider.'

Whitten heard the old campaigner behind him clear his throat. He offered no enlightment.

When they were roughly a mile from the fort with the sun sinking, that big bearded freighter sent one of his outriders to detach two wagons and kept right on going.

As the detail watched this Captain Morris frowned. He had never seen a train of wagons deliberately bypass a fort in isolated country, but his impression was that this wagon master was not a man who would waste time fraternising no matter how long he had been away from the company of others.

He shrugged and led his detail to the corrals to off saddle. Alan Whitten turned aside in the direction of his log house and could not have avoided hearing the freighters and the soldiers calling back and forth as the wagons crossed the compound. They, at least, seemed pleased to meet and exchange news and gossip as they lowered heavy tailgates and began unloading the two high-sided, wide-tyred wagons.

The empty wagons left the fort just short of sundown, and as the post gates were closed behind them, they made excellent time catching up with the wagons which had not stopped; they were riding light above their axles, the other wagons were not.

Alan Whitten heard the wood-cutting detail return as he was making supper, and later one of the other scouts, a 'breed known as Tom Crowfoot, came by to cadge a couple of swallows from Whitten's jug and exchange experiences. The wood-cutting detail had been scouted up by a couple of visible ragheads; there could have been more in hiding but the ones the detail saw were enough; everyone stopped loading, got weapons and waited, but the Indians had not re-appeared, and Tom Crowfoot laughed about that.

'Too many Spencer repeating rifles.'

Alan told the 'breed about the train of wagons. Tom Crowfoot dug out a foul little pipe, stuffed it with shag and eyed Whitten, whom he had known for several years. 'An' you don't like it,' he said, puffing up clouds of rank smelling smoke.

Whitten pushed the jug across the table but Tom Crowfoot ignored it. 'Charley Skinner?' he said. When Whitten nodded the 'breed removed his pipe, looked into its bowl and tamped the coals with a callused thumb-pad. 'Charley Skinner don't just outride.'

Al Whitten also pushed the jug aside. 'That's the story anyway. I wondered about it on the way back.'

Tom Crowfoot plugged the little pipe back between his teeth and regarded Whitten from very black eyes. 'They'll bivouac out there somewhere,' he said, and Whitten smiled across the table. 'You just got back.'

The 'breed showed strong white teeth in a grin. 'Didn't do much all day but ride with the wagons an' eat three times ... After dark?'

Al laughed. 'Damned In'ian mind reader,' he said, and after Tom Crowfoot left had another pull from the jug before returning it to its place behind the stove.

The sentry did not challenge them at the gate but he seemed reluctant to open up; no one had told him anyone would be leaving the post in the night. On the other hand scouts were privileged. They were also unpredictable. He opened the gate, stood a moment watching them ride west, closed, barred the gate and after a time of making his routine crossing back and forth, saw a tall, lean figure outlined by lamplight emerge from Captain Morris's hutment and sit on a chair out front in one of the first warm nights of the season.

He made two more passes across the gate, then resolutely crossed toward the seated silhouette still with his rifle on his shoulder, and said, 'Sir, Whitten an' that Crowfoot feller left the post ridin' west.'

Captain Morris regarded the soldier thoughtfully. 'Did they say anything?'

'Only that they had a chore to do.'

'Thanks,' the captain said, and watched the soldier return to his post.

Herbert Morris was not entirely unusual on the frontier, but after many years as a soldier, individuality had become fairly well submerged to discipline and routine.

He was curious about Whitten's departure, and most of the day he had been curious about something else: That wagon boss's unwillingness to stop at the post even long enough to rest his animals, get a free meal and relax for a few hours. He'd seen his share of supply trains and not once that he could recall had the teamsters neglected an opportunity to get a free meal and visit for a while.

As for Alan Whitten, while the captain's opinion was favorable, there were times when the scout was a riddle to him; like the way he hadn't just wanted to see how close he could get to the rim of Apache Canyon. As it turned out although Whitten had not said a word about it, he'd wanted to ascertain at considerable risk whether the Indians knew about the wagon train and were considering an attack upon it, which would have been evident in the pre-dawn by horse activity in the village.

And Whitten hadn't just taken Tom Crowfoot on a pleasure ride with him in the night. Not after both of them had put in hours of saddlebacking today, which suggested to Captain Morris they had something in mind which required darkness, nor had they wanted to tell him what their idea was, because either it was too sketchy in their own minds, or just as likely because they thought he would forbid them to leave the post.

Lieutenant Sorenson as officer of the day, supervised

changing of the guard and was on the way to his own hutment in full regalia, sword clanking and gauntlets tucked correctly under his garrison belt, when he saw the captain sitting there and turned aside.

'Nice night,' the lieutenant said, and leaned on one of the uprights of the tiny porch. 'The guard on the gate told me about Whitten and one of the 'breeds leaving.'

Captain Morris nodded.

'Did they get permission?' Sorenson asked, and also said, 'Not from me.'

The captain gazed in the direction of the massive wooden gate with its eight-foot bar in its hand-forged steel hangers. 'I didn't know about it until your sentry told me. As for permission ...'

'Major Burroughs won't like it, Captain.'

That was of course true. Major Burroughs did not like anything that departed from regulations. He was a good soldier and had been at a number of frontier posts, not all of which were operated to the precise Book of Army Regulations, and while they might have softened the spit-and-polish of some older officers, it had not had that affect on John Burroughs.

Sorenson straightened up to depart as he said, 'I'd better tell him.'

Captain Morris did not dispute this, but he said, 'Two scouts gone for a while, Eric, they aren't in the army.'

'But they have to obey regulations just like the rest of us. They get paid to do their jobs like we do.'

'Civilians,' said the captain, sounding almost mournful.

Lieutenant Sorenson looked down at the seated officer. 'Suppose they come back drunk as lords. They both drink, Captain.'

Morris made a gesture. 'Where? Not out there, Eric. They've got jugs cached in their cabins ... The major doesn't like to be awakened late at night.'

'I should let it go until morning?'

'I can't tell you what to do, not in this case, all I can tell you is that I've been in charge of scouts in different places for a long time. They've all been the same in some ways, one of which is that unless ordered to do otherwise, they pretty much come and go as they please.'

Lieutenant Sorenson said, 'Good night,' and went clanking toward his own hutment. The decision to do nothing right now had not been hard for him to make. He placed a world of value on Captain Morris's ideas, and whether others felt the same way or not, Eric Sorenson was unshakably convinced that someday Captain Morris would have his own command somewhere, if not in some god-forsaken fort in the middle of nowhere, then back east where the pay was better, living conditions were pleasant, and damned army scouts did not exist.

The captain took his problem to bed with him, and having never had much trouble sleeping, had no difficulty sleeping on this night.

It was not until the next morning as he was heading for breakfast and saw no smoke rising from Alan Whitten's stovepipe that he veered in the direction of the area where the scouts lived and went around back. One of Whitten's horses was gone. He went to the next log house and looked in Tom Crowfoot's corral. Where there should have been two horses there was one.

He went thoughtfully to the mess hall, ate in silence and afterwards went to the major's officer where he found the commanding officer with a cup of coffee standing beside the desk where his orderly usually sat.

The major gestured with his coffee cup. 'On sick list. It's the end of the month with reports to be made an' he's on sick list.'

Captain Morris brushed that aside. 'Two scouts left last night and haven't returned.'

'Left? How do you mean – left?'

'They rode out the gate.'

Major Burroughs put his cup down carefully. 'With whose permission, Captain?'

'As far as I know, Major, without permission. They certainly didn't get it from me.'

The major's short temper came up. 'Gawdammit! Scouts! For all the good they do they might just as well never been hired.'

That was hardly true but Captain Morris stood stoically silent.

'Rode out ... What about the sentry on the gate?'

'Sir, scouts pretty much come and go as they please, unless they're told to stay inside the fort. It wasn't the sentry's fault.'

'Whitten?'

'Yes sir. And Tom Crowfoot.'

'Son of a bitch! Where would they go; what possible reason ... unless they've got a whiskey cache out there somewhere.'

It was against regulations for anyone to have liquor on the post. But that had never been applied with any severity to civilians on the post, not even the ones in government service.

'Whitten drinks, Captain. That's a known fact!'

'Major, I've known him for several years and not once have I seen him drunk or even close to it.'

'Captain, I've heard ...'

'You can hear anything, Sir. You could even hear that I drink or that Lieutenant Sorenson ...'

'Why the hell are you defending him, Captain? He left the post without permission!'

'Major, I'm simply reporting what I know.'

'Well, damn it, when they return send Whitten to me.'

'Sir ... They've been gone all night.'

'Drunk and asleep somewhere out there.'

'Sir, I'd like your permission to go find them.'

Major Burroughs retrieved his coffee cup and looked gloomily at the orderly's vacant chair. His reply was

almost off hand. 'All right. And when you get back bring
them to my office ... Now where in the hell am I going
to find another orderly!'

# THREE
## Chains

Springtime nights were long. Not as long as winter nights but close enough. What helped somewhat to dispel long dark hours was moonlight, which was only reliable if men set their nocturnal habits by when it would be brightest.

The night Alan Whitten and Tom Crowfoot rode west of Fort Winfield Scott there was half a moon and a million stars. The light was better than total darkness but not very much.

What made it easier for them was four of those freight rigs had been loaded to the axles and left tracks three inches wide a child could have followed, daylight or dark.

After an hour of riding Tom Crowfoot wagged his head. Freight wagons were snail-paced even when empty, when loaded as these wagons had been they were lucky to make two miles an hour.

But after riding for a solid hour when there was still no sound of wagons, nor signs of a campfire, Crowfoot said, 'Who is the wagon master?'

All Alan Whitten could offer in reply was a general discription of a large bearded man and make an observation that had gradually come to him. 'If he don't slack off he's going to end up with some horses too tuckered to pull.'

Crowfoot raised an arm. A distant flicker of firelight appeared in the darkness. 'He kept goin' longer than I would have, if those wagons was as loaded as you said.'

Whitten was watching the light when he replied. 'They were as loaded, Tom.'

'Now what do we do?' Crowfoot asked.

'Scout 'em up.'

A fair distance east of the fire they tied their animals among some lodgepole pines and went ahead on foot. The 'breed was willing but puzzled. 'What are we doing?'

Whitten's answer did not help. 'Damned if I know, but with Skinner as an outrider and that furry-faced wagon master pushing harder than most would do, I'm just plain curious.,'

Crowfoot walked silently beside his companion looking more baffled than worried. When Alan Whitten hissed and halted, Crowfoot saw the armed sentry leaning on a man-high rear wagon wheel rolling a smoke. He was not particularly impressed; in hostile country only fools did not keep sentries out and around.

But when Whitten pointed in two other directions, each about a hundred feet from the man making the smoke, Crowfoot scowled, leaned and whispered, 'Maybe they know something we don't know. Maybe they know ragheads are goin' to hit 'em.'

Alan was pondering. Six wagons meant at least twelve men, a driver and swamper for each wagon. If there were other outriders, including Skinner and that bronco who had been riding with him, there could be upwards of fifteen, maybe twenty men with the train.

He led off trying to get somewhere that wagons did not interfere with a sighting of the fire. The best he could do was find a blind spot among the surround of sentries where one wagon tongue had not been run beneath the wagon ahead of it, and slip in there where he had a good sighting of the fire and the men around it.

Crowfoot let his breath out slowly.

Whitten's best estimate had been far too low. Assuming those guards were completely around the wagons as they appeared to be, there were half again as many men with the train as Al had guessed; there were nine men around the fire and one more out a ways bringing wood to the ring of stones around the fire.

Crowfoot leaned to whisper, 'That's a lot of men for just six wagons. You know any of them?'

Whitten shook his head as the man with the armload of wood came up, dropped his load and turned aside to expectorate before taking his place among the other men around the fire.

Whitten searched out the big bearded wagon master and found him sitting like an Indian with an earthen jug between his legs.

Conversation was sporadic and revealed only the interest of the men at the fire with how much longer they had to travel before they got to the Burnt Timbers settlement, and the bewhiskered man gruffly said, 'Another day. We'd ought to pull in there tomorrow night.'

A man whose back was to Whitten and Crowfoot addressed the big burly man. 'Ira, I told you back yonder we got to rest the horses.'

The bearded man replied indifferently. 'All they got to do is stay up in their collars one more day. That's all.'

The man with his back to Whitten and the 'breed was apparently more stubborn than prudent. 'They was draggin' when we stopped tonight. An overnight rest on poor graze ain't goin' to be enough.'

For the second time Alan Whitten had seen him, the big man demonstrated a quick temper, a short fuse and an impatient disposition.

'Curtis, I told you – told all of you – we was goin' to push hard. If it hadn't been for those two loads for the army post we could have been even farther along.' He then made a statement that made the two scouts stare at him. 'I was against goin' anywhere near that army fort.'

Whitten looked over his shoulder and began
withdrawing back out into the night. When they were
safely away he told Tom Crowfoot he smelled carrion
and the 'breed nodded.

The sentries were moving, pacing around the wagons
at their spaced intervals, and each one of them was
carrying a carbine, not unusual under the circumstances
– this was Apache country – but so many sentries
implied to Alan Whitten something he may have long
suspected but until tonight in the gloom around the
wagon camp, had not squarely faced. 'I want to look
inside those wagons,' he told the 'breed, and Tom
Crowfoot ran a gaze over where the wagons stood, with
a sentry for each wagon. 'Did you see Charley Skinner at
the fire?'

'No.'

'Neither did I.'

'That worries you, Tom?'

'It don't make me real happy, Alan.'

They hovered until the sentries were back to loafing
by their wagons, watched a particular man who was tall,
thin as a rail and could have had lice because he
constantly removed his hat to vigorously scratch.

This sentry did not lean as the others did, he sank to
the ground with his back to a large wheel and alternately
scratched and yawned.

Tom said, 'We got all night.'

They got belly down to watch the tired man with his
back to a big wheel. It was a long wait. Once the sentry
climbed to his feet when another man came around, and
this time Whitten recognised Charley Skinner. In poor
light his smoke-tans looked light, almost pearl grey. But
even if he hadn't been wearing buckskin his size would
have identified him. He was no more than average
height but his thickness could only be matched among
the teamsters by the man at the fire called Ira. Charley
Skinner was several inches shorter than Ira, who was as

large as any of them, larger than most, and also built like a bull.

The tired sentry and Skinner exchanged words briefly before Skinner walked over to the next wagon. Crowfoot said 'Lucky that feller wasn't asleep ... I've seen smaller trains than this one put out only two or three guards.'

Whitten nodded. 'What's in the wagons, Tom?'

'I got no idea, but whatever it is they sure don't aim to have anyone scout them up, do they?'

Whitten watched the tired man yawn and slide down the wheel again. He might drift off, and then again he might not do this for an hour or two.

As Tom has said, they had all night, but Whitten's decision was not to wait for something as unpredictable as that sentry dozing off.

They were in a hurry, which was in their favour. When Alan had the routine of those guards pretty well understood he nudged Tom and they began their second stalk toward the wagons, but this time toward a particular wagon. They probably could have got close enough without that drowsy guard; they were both experienced at this sort of thing, but it was almost too easy.

Al hesitated within fifteen feet of the guard but Tom nudged him and shook his head. Crowfoot's reasoning was sound; if they knocked the damned fool over the head, the next time Skinner made his round he would find, not a sleeping sentry but an unconscious one.

It was not simply a matter of climbing into the wagon; they still had to climb out and get back to their horses.

The front of the wagon had a water barrel lashed to the near side and the binder handle was fully forward locking the rear wheels in place. Like most handles this one had a short rope hanging from it so that in an emergency a man on foot or horseback could grab the rope and yank it until the binders stopped rear wheels from moving.

They used the short rope to climb soundlessly to the boot behind and above which was the wooden seat, and behind that was the tightly puckered canvas. Crowfoot's knife moved, the pucker string parted and the canvas sagged.

It was darker inside the wagon than a well, but with eyes accustomed to little light, Whitten and Crowfoot beheld all they had to see.

Boxes of ammunition stacked and lashed so they would not slide and jumble over rough ground, and what held both scouts motionless and almost breathless for a space of seconds, a Gatling gun with its wheels in place, fully operational, its multiple barrels pointing toward the tailgate.

Crowfoot started to whisper but Whitten raised a hand for absolute silence. He turned to climb back over the seat with Crowfoot behind him.

The camp was silent, the fire was dying, the night had advanced only a fraction since they'd climbed in, and as they started to climb down to the ground a quiet, soft voice said, 'Right where you are!'

They froze beside one another with their backs to the wagon. For a long moment there was not a sound and no visible movement. The man coming toward them from the west side of the next wagon was thick, dressed in pale buckskin and was holding a dragoon revolver in his right hand.

He stopped and spoke in the same quiet voice. 'All right, lads.' Other men stepped from hiding but only one or two started toward the scouts. The foremost of these men was large, bearded and massively put together. He walked to within ten feet and cocked his sidearm.

Even under different circumstances it would have been clear that this man was one of those no-nonsense individuals lacking in humour and other human saving graces.

Skinner sauntered closer, let his handgun hang at his side and stonily regarded Alan Whitten, whom he recognised from their earlier meeting. Skinner seemed to be turning something over in his mind and when the bearded man slowly and with unmistakable purpose raised his cocked sidearm, Skinner said, 'If there's more of 'em, a gunshot will bring 'em on the run.'

The big man lowered his weapon but did not ease down the hammer.

Skinner nodded at Whitten. 'You were with the army detail. I remember you. Who's the 'breed?'

'Friend of mine,' Whitten replied.

'Must be to let you lead him into an ambush, mister … What's your name?'

'Alan Whitten.'

'Civilian scout for the fort back yonder.' He turned to the glowering bearded man, 'If they're alone we're all right.'

'If,' the bearded man snarled. 'Go make sure, Charley. Just you; one man can scout better'n a lot of men. We'll talk to these two by the fire. One damned fact; we got to settle this quick and get to rollin' again.'

The man named Curtis who had protested in favour of the horses before, snorted and rolled his eyes but wisely said nothing.

Skinner lingered. 'Whitten?'

'Yes.'

'How'd you come to sneak into that wagon?'

'Curious.'

'Them teamsters that unloaded at the fort said something?'

'No. This is the first train I ever saw that wouldn't stop for a meal and some rest.'

'Who's out there with you?'

Whitten was tempted to lie but Tom Crowfoot said, 'No one. We come out here on our own.'

The bearded man snarled and Skinner checked him up. 'I'll look around, but if there's others they'll be wondering what's takin' these two so long … They might be tellin' the truth. Scouts got a habit of sneakin' around on their own.'

As Skinner was leathering his handgun and turning away the bearded man said, 'Be careful; if they're out there they'll hear you. Ambushes work both ways, Charley.'

Skinner smiled at the bearded man, 'Give 'em some coffee, Ira. Whether there's anyone out there or not these two won't be around come sunrise.'

Ira and his companions herded their captives over where someone tossed in wood to make the coals spring to life. As they sat on the ground, silent and thoughtful, undoubtedly worried as well, a man who looked and dressed like a stockman, spoke in a nasal voice. 'What'd you see in the wagon?'

'Ammunition and a Gatling gun,' stated Alan Whitten.

The cattleman did not blink an eye. 'How long you been in Apacheria?'

Tom Crowfoot answered, 'Me, about six years. Alan about the same time at Fort Scott and at other posts.'

The cattleman spread his hands palms downward as he resumed speaking. 'Well then, you boys know about the massacre at Burnt Timbers a while back. Me, I wasn't there at the time. I drove in a herd of beef the following year.' The cowman ignored Ira, whose menacing figure was highlighted by the re-kindled fire. Not for a moment did the large bearded man take his eyes off Whitten and Crowfoot.

'What you got to face up to,' the cowman said, 'is that this ain't a real kindly countryside. Hell, there's 'Paches not thirty miles from here in a damned canyon. Them little bastards got no rules, they kill on sight, steal, plunder, burn, torture folks. They shoot cattle just for the hell of it. Where I come from they got Comanches, birds of a feather with ragheads. They shoot cattle by the hundreds; no reason, they don't take the meat, don't like the taste of beef. Kill 'em to hurt stockmen ... Now then, folks got a right to defend themselves wouldn't you say?'

Whitten was silent. He was beginning to have a dawning suspicion.

The cowman turned to big, bearded Ira. 'You can sure have 'em, Mister Blakely, unless they figure to come to their senses. One way or another it ain't goin' to change anything.'

Charley Skinner returned with a Winchester in the crook of one arm. He sat down with all eyes on him, and smiled craftily across the fire at Whitten and Crowfoot. 'Brought your horses back with me,' he said, sounding satisfied with himself.

Ira did not like anything that was not practical and frank. 'Who'd you find? How many?'

'None, Ira. Just where these fellers left their horses. Backtracked enough in poor light to know they came out here alone.'

The relief of the men at the fire was almost palpable. The man named Curtis who had tried to get better treatment for the teams, looked over at Ira as he said, 'Alone or not, by the time we get to Burnt Timbers an' unload, the soldiers are goin' to miss these two.'

Ira glowered. 'You got somethin' better?'

'Yes. Unload the damned guns and ammunition right here and get the hell ...'

The cowman exploded. 'You get paid for deliverin' the supplies at Burnt Timbers. You leave them out here in the middle of open country and we won't give you a red cent.' His flash of temper passed, his voice dropped back to its normal tone. 'Get the wagons rolling right now. Keep goin' an' you'll be in Burnt Timbers by tomorrow afternoon.'

Curtis shook his head at the rancher. 'An' with the damned army breathin' down our necks. Ira ...'

The big bearded man grumbled. 'The wagons will

roll. If the army comes we'll have these two sons of
bitches to trade to 'em for clear passage out of the
damned country. Or we'll stand 'em on a tailgate where
everyone can see 'em, and cut their throats ... Charley?'

Skinner nodded in emphatic approval.

There were other stockmen at the fire. Alan finally
had an idea why there had been more men at this
wagon-camp than there had been when the wagons had
passed Fort Scott. Riders from Burnt Timbers had met
the wagons out here.

One man offered an alternative course of action.
Evidently he had not liked what Ira had said and
Charley Skinner had approved of. It was one thing to
sneak Gatling guns into a town, and another thing to kill
men who were connected with the army. The country he
and others killed in was not a state, it was a territory, and
US possessions called territories were administered by
the army, not civilians.

Clearly, in this stockman's opinion getting caught
sneaking in proscribed rapid-fire guns was marginally
moral at best, but deliberately committing murder to do
it, was something else.

He said, 'Take 'em along as hostages, but don't kill
them. The army'll never let up if we do that. Never.' He
looked among the solemn faces before adding a little
more. 'We use the guns to wipe out the ragheads like we
planned, but that's different; even the army wants to do
that.'

Whitten, who had been staring at this cattleman when
he first began speaking, thought there was one troubled
cattleman who might help them, then the rancher had
said the rest of it and Whitten's stare widened.

They wanted those rapid-fire guns not to defend their
ranches and their town, they meant to take them down
to Apache Canyon.

There certainly were people who would not have
faulted wholesale slaughter of the kind Gatling guns

dealt out, but Alan Whitten was not one of them. He had fought Indians, had felt thoroughly justified when he had been attacked by them; a man had the right to defend his life, but what that particular cowman was talking about was not defence, it was offence of the most grisly variety.

Apache Canyon was full of women and children, old people who were harmless, and the man cranking a Gatling gun would not, could not in fact, differentiate if he wanted to. If he did not want to there would be an unparalleled massacre.

Skinner asked Ira where the jug was. Ira jutted his jaw toward the wood pile. When Skinner returned and passed the jug around, Ira glared when a teamster sitting next to Tom Crowfoot seemed about to hand the jug to the 'breed. 'Don't waste it,' he snarled. 'Where they're goin' they won't need whiskey.'

Skinner jack-knifed up to his feet. 'If we're goin' to roll these two better be chained out of sight in a wagon ... On your feet Whitten, and your smoke-tanned friend.'

He took them to a wagon with a higher seat than the others, got them inside over the tailgate and pointed to a pile of loose chains as he drew and cocked his sidearm. 'Mister Whitten, you make damned sure you chain that 'breed real good. Ankles first then arms behind his back. Use them clevis bolts to lock him in.'

Alan went to work. Tom sat stoically looking past Skinner to the blue-black tranquillity of space. When he had been made helpless Charley Skinner motioned for Whitten to step away. Charley inserted his pistol barrel into the clevis bolt and gave it a hard twist. Crowfoot would be unable to free himself without something equally strong to be inserted into the bolt to loosen it.

Skinner motioned for Alan to lie belly-down. He holstered his sixgun and unwound more chain from the pile. As he was lashing Whitten's ankles he said, 'How long before you'll be missed at the fort?'

Alan thought maybe six hours but he said, 'Not too long. They got a good sentry system; it checks on everyone's bed every hour or so.'

Skinner finished with Alan's arms behind his back and stood up. 'Somethin' I think I ought to tell you boys: If the army comes up and gets rank, two of them Gatlings is loaded and ready to fire.'

Whitten started upwards. 'You'd be crazy to do that,' he said.

Skinner shrugged as he made his way toward the high tailgate. 'Be crazier if we didn't do it, them guns being illegal to civilians and all. Out here where no one but maybe a coyote would hear, we could hide the carcasses, take the horses with us, off-load at Burnt Timbers and head south for maybe two, three, four days before anyone figured out what happened.'

Skinner went over the tailgate and left a lingering sound of scornful laughter in his wake.

Whitten looked at Tom Crowfoot. 'Got any slack? I left a little.'

'Not after that bastard twisted the bolt tight ... Al, they're crazy. Downright plumb crazy. Never in this world will they get away with it.'

Whitten said, 'Right now, Tom, I'm not worrying about them, I'm worring about us.'

'You got any slack?'

'No, and this isn't rope we could gnaw through.'

# FOUR
# A Very Long Day

When Charley Skinner returned to the fire the others were glum. He sat down, looked around and said, 'The army'll come lookin' for them two.'

No one disputed this, a couple of the Burnt Timbers cattlemen nodded, otherwise there was neither agreement nor disagreement.

Skinner smiled. 'Two guns is loaded and ready.'

That remark brought every eye to Skinner, who continued to smile. 'We unlimber the guns on 'em.'

Several men gasped and Ira's brows dropped ominously. 'We'll deliver the guns, Charley, but we ain't goin' to war with the army.'

Skinner held his smile. 'Won't be any need, Ira,' he replied. 'We kill 'em, chase off their horses an leave barefoot horse tracks. Apaches ambushed the troopers. Hell, it's been goin' on like that for thirty years. Ragheads are the best bushwhackers in the trade. We gather up their guns, toss 'em in one of the wagons an' there you got it: Exactly like Apaches would do.'

For a long time there was not a word spoken. Ira handed the jug around and everyone took a swallow of Dutch courage. Afterwards that stockman with the whiney voice broke the silence.

'Ira ...?'

The surly bearded man cleared his throat but made

no comment.

Skinner looked around and settled on one of the cowmen to ask his opinion. This time the whiskey'd had time to work, 'Well,' the rancher said. 'One thing is a cinch; if the army believes ragheads ambushed and wiped out soldiers, we won't have to go down there and clean 'em out with the Gatling guns, will we?'

Several men left the fire to seek their blankets. There were only four remaining by the time the jug made another round, and one of those was the whiney-voiced cowman who said, 'Except for them damned scouts we wouldn't be in this fix.'

Skinner's retort was blunt. 'They're here, friend. It don't do no good bellyachin' over spilt milk. They come, we caught 'em, and it's no longer just delivering your guns and the ammunition. We got to figure ahead.'

The whiney-voiced man expressed uneasiness. 'But the US army, for chrissake.'

Ira was silent for a long time before speaking in a way that left no doubt he was coming down on Skinner's side. 'We didn't do it, the ragheads did. We can leave plenty sign around to convince the army. Now then – we better harness up and get to rolling.'

The teamster named Curtis did not protest, probably because he knew it would have been useless, but when he arose to go out to bring in some horses he wagged his head. Since passing the fort back yonder he had been very conscious of the condition of his draft animals.

The camp was routed out, Whitten and Crowfoot heard the noise and knew what was happening. Crowfoot said, 'Well; at least we'll see another sunrise.' He paused and grinned at Al Whitten. 'But I wouldn't bet a speckled pony we'll see another one after that.'

Whitten had tested his chains, as with Crowfoot, there was slack, which, with rope, would have been encouraging, but with chains secured by clevis bolts it simply signified that chains could not be pulled as taut as rope.

He held his head off the wagon bed long enough to hear someone climbing heavily to the seat out front. A hard-faced man looked in at them and said, 'Which one of you cut the pucker string?' When he got no answer he cursed, straightened around, kicked off the binder and whistled up his hitch.

The wagon had no springs, but even if it'd been made with them the ride would not have been much easier, just more liable to sway over bumpy places than to jolt over them.

Whitten rolled over and jack-knifed into a sitting position, which made the chain running from his ankles to his wrist tighten. Crowfoot tried the same manoeuvre but his chain had more slack in it. They looked at each other, and Crowfoot smiled.

'My aunt wanted me to live on the reservation,' he said, and Whitten smiled back. 'You should have listened to her.'

The wagon they were in had boxes of ammuntion but no Gatling gun. It also had boxes of camp food including several sacks of flour. It was not as low on its axles as the wagons with Gatling guns in them.

Tom Crowfoot eyed the sacks of flour, looked elsewhere then returned his gaze to the flour sacks. Eventually, he tumble-crawled until his back was to one of them. Tom Whitten said, 'Like a feather bed?'

Crowfoot did not reply. He stared through slitted eyes at the loose canvas beyond which he could see the broad back of the teamster. He did not take his eyes off the man as he made repeated attempts to puncture one of the sacks. The cloth was cross-grained and thick. He had to give up using a rigid thumb in favour of a link of his chain, and even then he achieved success only after he was sweating from the effort.

Alan Whitten watched without any idea what the 'breed was up to, and Crowfoot worked without looking at his companion.

Once, when a wagon up ahead halted which made all the wagons behind it stop, the teamster twisted to look back to make sure the captives were helpless, before climbing down to hike forward and help remove the spare wheel under another wagonbed and bolt it in place of one that had caused the delay when three spokes broke under the load of an over-burdened wagon.

It required time to jack the disabled wagon off the ground, free the hub-nut, which resisted being removed, pull off the useless wheel, roll it aside and hoist the sound one into its place, tighten the hub nut and lower the ratchet jack.

When the teamster returned, kicked off his brake and evened-up his lines he spoke gruffly over his shoulder. 'It'll happen every time you over-load 'em.' As he whistled up his hitch he also said, 'Well, the horses needed the rest. Horses ain't machines, but tryin' to get that into someone's brain in this haul is like spittin' in the ocean.'

Al thought their teamster was the man named Curtis who had been protesting about the condition of the animals. He was right but it would be a while before he could verify it.

Crowfoot was slumped against his flour sack, sweaty and raw-nerved. He still avoided Whitten's quizzical gaze. In fact he rolled back on the flour sack and closed his eyes.

It was cold inside the old wagon, and when pre-dawn's lustreless fish-belly colour brightened the world in grudging degrees, it got even colder.

The teamster looped both lines around the binder handle and shrugged into a shapeless old woollen coat, freed the lines and drove on.

They stopped after sunrise to rest the animals and Charley Skinner climbed in. He was wearing a flesh-side out sheepskin coat, looked in need of a shave, and hunkered near Al Whitten, evidently in a good mood as he said, 'Well now, gents, I thought I ought to tell you. In case you're expecting the army to track you, I took both your horses out a ways back yonder, looped a rein through each cheekpiece and set 'em loose, so's anyone trackin' 'em will go off northeasterly on the trail of two shod-horses goin' along side by side like fellers was riding them.'

Crowfoot was roused out of sleep by Skinner's voice. He listened, then sank back on his flour sack. Al Whitten said, 'You got a bag of tricks, haven't you?'

Skinner smiled. 'You got no idea, Mister Whitten. A man's got to learn a lot of tricks to get by in this life.'

Skinner offered Whitten a chew from a lint-encrusted plug and shrugged when the scout shook his head. After tucking the cud into his cheek he asked when Whitten had eaten last, and shook his head over the reply. 'Chawin' tobacco ain't no substitute for meat an' potatoes, but it's better 'n nothing at all.'

Skinner was in a relaxed mood and Al Whitten responded to that by asking whether the hitches would last all the way to Burnt Timbers.

Skinner's answer riled the man out front on the high seat. When he said, 'They'll hold out because they got to.' The teamster craned around. 'If they last half way I'll eat my hat.'

Skinner eyed the teamster for a moment, then turned his back on him to address Al Whitten again. 'How many soldiers at that log fort?'

'Sixty, mounted and foot … They'll be along. I'm surprised they haven't shown up already.'

Skinner smiled. 'In your fix, scout, I'd worry about that too.' His smile faded. 'If they do, you better pray they'll trade for you to leave us alone until we get to the Burnt Timbers settlement.'

Whitten's brow crinkled. 'What good will it do for you to reach Burnt Timbers if the army's behind you?'

'Well, Mister Whitten, my notion is to settle with the soldiers before we reach the settlement.'

As they looked steadily at one another for a moment, a horseman rode up to the tailgate and yelled for Charley Skinner to come up front. Ira Blakely wanted him.

Before leaving, the man in the smoke-tans tapped Whitten lightly on the shoulder. 'Are you a prayin' man? If you are pray them soldiers follow the trail of your two horses.'

After Skinner climbed out of the wagon and the teamster was preparing to whistle up his hitch after its rest, Tom Crowfoot stared at Alan Whitten. So softly the teamster could not hear him over the creaking and groaning of his wagon in motion, Crowfoot said, 'You know what I think?'

Al Whitten nodded. 'Yeah, I think so.'

'The patrol won't be very big. Maybe these bastards will just try bluffin' past them.

'Tom, maybe they won't even come after the wagons. Did you hear what he said about using our horses tied tandem to leave a false trail? The patrol will be lookin' for us. They got no reason to suspect anything's wrong with these wagons.'

Crowfoot eased back on his flour sack and made an enigmatic comment. 'Who's the best sign reader at Fort Scott?'

'You.'

'No. Everett Tanyard.'

Whitten continued to gaze at Crowfoot, but the 'breed eased back on his flour sack and closed his eyes.

Al knew the third Ford Scott scout, Everett Tanyard, who was no more than a third whiteskin, looked totally Indian and was pretty much of a loner. When they had first met he'd been intrigued by the dark man's name but waited until he and Tom Crowfoot were on a scout to ask about it. Crowfoot's reply would have made perfect sense to most tribesmen. Everett's mother had been taken with birthing pains at some settlement, and had her baby behind a tanyard that smelled terrible and was infested with fat blue-tailed flies. She had named her baby boy for the place where she'd birthed him. Nothing unusual about that. At the time Tom had explained this Al Whitten had wondered why she hadn't named her baby Blue-Tail Fly. He'd never been within smelling distance of a tanyard that those shiny big flies hadn't been around in droves.

The teamster spoke gruffly again over his shoulder. 'Riders comin' from the southeast.' He had no sooner made that announcement than Charley Skinner and his Indian companion loped away from the train toward those distant horsemen.

From his position deeper in the wagon Tom Crowfoot called to the teamster. 'Soldiers?'

The teamster laughed. 'No, they ain't all dressed the same but from here I can' tell much except that there's six or seven of 'em ... Hell! Charley's bring them back with him.'

Alan Whitten's spirits rose a little but not very much. Springtime in open country brought forth all manner of people from settlers to pot-hunters to ragheads. At least these would not be Apaches.

The teamster spoke again. 'Hunters. They got rifles instead of carbines.'

He was correct, but Ira, who had already identified the strangers for what they were, did not stop the wagons. He sent a rider back to tell Skinner to get rid of the hunters, not to bring them back to the wagons with him, and this became clear when the teamster called again. 'They're palavering ... The hunters is turning east. Skinner most likely told 'em he saw a band of bufflers or something over there ... They ain't goin't to be real pleased; haven't been any sizable bands of game out here in years. Never was any buffler that I ever saw.'

Al Whitten guessed the teamster was in a talkative mood so he said, 'Good thing it wasn't a band of ragheads,' and the teamster chuckled about that. 'I was sort of hopin' it would be.'

He said no more and neither did Whitten.

Heat came into the new day, Crowfoot asked if the teamster had a canteen. The man twisted, unslung a canteen and tossed it back. Both Tom and Al drank their fill and Whitten pushed the half-empty canteen as far forward as he could with his feet. The teamster retrieved it, gazed at them a moment, then said, 'If you lads'd used your heads last night you wouldn't be chained up today. Charley Skinner's got eyes in the back of his head. When he found that sleepin' sentry he got real close, listened to you in the wagon, and snuck away to organise a welcomin' committee.'

How they had been caught interested them both a lot less than what lay ahead for them, but the teamster either did not know or did not want to say. He straightened back around, re-slung his canteen and hunched forward in pleasant heat, concentrating on his hitch.

The heat came slowly into the wagon, but once it arrived it continued to build up. Canvas wagon-covers acted like reflectors not buffers.

Crowfoot slept right up until they made another rest halt, when the customary jolting awakened him by its lack.

Al Whitten had dozed off and on but had never really slept. When the wagons halted again he called to the teamster. 'We can't be at Burnt Timbers yet, can we?'

There was no response because the driver had climbed down and walked ahead where other men were gathering at a lowered tailgate for their noon-day meal.

During the teamster's absence Tom Crowfoot got that far-away look of concentration on his face. Al Whitten watched, wondered, but knew better than to ask questions. If Crowfoot had wanted him to know the other time they stopped and he sat bolt upright staring into the distance, he would have told him.

They had halted near a busy little willow-creek where trout minnows exploded in all directions when horse heads appeared to drink.

Charley Skinner seemed untroubled but Ira Blakely did not. He asked several of the stockmen who were riding alongside the wagons how much farther, and each time he got a different answer, but they were within a mile or two of one another.

One cowman said six miles, another said eight miles and the third man said seven miles.

Ira told Charley Skinner they would not have to push the hitches from here on. It was a little past mid-day and without straining the train could reach the settlement about sundown, which was already beginning to take a little longer and it wasn't even full summer yet.

Whether Skinner was pleased about this announcement, the man standing next to him wolfing down food, was pleased, and evidently Ira knew it because he said, 'All right, Curtis, from here on we baby the damned horses.'

Curtis was drinking coffee and had nothing to say, but he bobbed his head in approval.

When he returned to his wagon, got settled and ready to roll, Tom Crowfoot called to him. 'You fellers short of grub?'

The teamster did not answer until he had his hitch moving again, then all he said was: 'You're Charley's prisoners, not mine,' but evidently it bothered him that the chained men had not been fed, so the next time Skinner rode past he called to him that the captives were hungry.

The response he got did not seem to surprise him. 'No hurry about that. They'll get fed this evening.'

The teamster watched Skinner lope away and growled

more to himself than to Crowfoot or Whitten, but they both heard him.

'You either never been hungry, Charley, or you've forgot what it's like.'

Whitten called for the canteen again and this time when he kicked it forward it was empty. The teamster up-ended it, wagged his head and re-slung it. 'Hot back there, eh,' he said. 'I was in the commissary department durin' the war. I know what it's like under a full spread of canvas on a hot day.'

Whitten's reply was almost sarcastic. 'I thought you'd been in the artillery.'

The teamster craned around, glared and sat forward. There was no more conversation for a long time.

Crowfoot slept, Whitten tried to; he napped off and on but they were passing over rough ground. Each lunge or lurch snapped him wide awake.

He speculated about the situation back at Fort Scott; by now everyone knew he and Tom Crowfoot were missing. His guess was that Captain Morris, in charge of civilian scouts, would be searching for them with a patrol, and that notion brought another one: Everett Tanyard would be with the patrol; he'd been the only scout left, and he would pick up Whitten and Tom Crowfoot's tracks, follow them, and go riding off in the wrong direction as Charley Skinner had planned.

He was napping when the teamster said, 'I told Charley if he didn't feed you I was goin' to cut you loose.'

Al shook his head about that. Charley Skinner was not a man to give ultimatums to, but Al Whitten did not know the teamster named Curtis Somethingorother.

He had his first inkling that the teamster was not just another freighter when Charley rode up alongside on horseback and flung a bag of jerky over into the boot at Curtis's feet, and rode away without a word.

The teamster twisted, flung the sack back and gruffly

said, 'Gnaw through the bag if you're hungry,' and sat forward again, evidently satisfied he had done his duty, which did not include doing any more.

Crowfoot left his flour sack and inched up where Al was tearing the sack. It was awkward, even a little painful to eat belly-down and chained, but hunger made these inconveniences bearable.

They chewed jerky for more than an hour. One thing about jerky was the longer a man chewed it the bigger it got as it absorbed saliva. Another thing about it was that, having been cured with salt and pepper, it was not very long after a man ate it that he got very thirsty.

The teamster solved this last problem by looping his lines, leaving his hitch to follow the wagon ahead while he lifted the lid off the barrel lashed to the near-side, pushed the canteen into tepid water until it was full, and tossed it back where Whitten and Crowfoot waited.

They had trouble again. Drinking from a canteen without hands to hold it was not only difficult, but if the teamster hadn't filled the canteen to its gullet, they would not have been able to slack their thirst before what they spilled emptied the canteen.

But there was a blessing too; spilled water dried slowly off their clothing, making them feel almost pleasantly cool.

# FIVE
# Dissention

As before, when the teamster saw riders, he called to the men inside the wagon. 'Welcomin' committee. Can't see no rooftops but we got to be pretty close.'

It was late afternoon. According to Whitten's estimate they should be within sight of their destination.

As before, Charley Skinner and his Indian companion rode out to meet the newcomers, and the teamster was right. But what Charley brought them back with him this time was Burnt Timbers townsmen, not another band of cattle ranchers. The teamster, with nothing else to watch, eased back against his seat and sounded relieved when he said, 'Well now; wasn't that neighbourly, them comin' out to meet the wagons.'

He hadn't sounded sarcastic but he could have been. The newcomers, along with the scouts and ranchers who had ridden to meet them, led the way back, and although it might have been expected that Ira would halt, he kept right on driving as the newcomers warped in beside his rig and carried on a brief conversation, then dropped back with Skinner and his Indian.

One of them was a man nearly as large as Ira and he was not pleased at the reception. He told Charley Skinner that Blakely did not seem very amiable, and Charley mentioned the captive scouts in one of the wagons, and the possibilty that an army detail was looking for them.

The big cowman halted his horse and stared. Behind him several of his companions made unhappy noises. But it was one voice, pitched higher than the others, who put their dismay into words.

'You was supposed to get them damned guns to Burnt Timbers without no one knowing.'

Skinner told the truth. 'We didn't stop at the fort. Until we stopped for supper an' I found them scouts from the fort trackin' us we didn't have nothin' to worry about.'

The irate townsman was not mollified. 'Let's go up an' talk to Blakely, an' this time he better stop his wagon.'

Whitten and Crowfoot heard none of this but their teamster had, and he groaned, leaned forward and glowered glumly at the rising and falling rumps of his horses. Once, after the entire train had halted and the teamster climbed down, the chained men inside heard someone shout. Crowfoot tried to roll close enough to see under the wagon canvas. He could not do it after he got over there but he was not disheartened.

'Them townsmen are upset. Maybe they seen a patrol from the fort.'

Al Whitten did not reply, but he thought the halt probably had nothing to do with Fort Scott.

Crowfoot got back over against his flower sack and leaned there seeming in anticipation of some grand moment. Al Whitten did not have the heart to make doubting comments so he kept quiet.

When the teamster returned he acted disgusted. He climbed to his seat but did not unloop the lines, he instead took his time getting a sliver of molasses cured into his cheek, then he turned to squint down inside the wagon as he said, 'I had a bad feelin' right from the start.'

When Al asked him what had gone wrong he turned his back on the captives and glowered at the rumps of his horses until Charley Skinner came down the line, halted, exchanged a look with the teamster and said, 'Well, that was like flint on steel. That big feller on horseback's named James Fanning. Him and Ira hit it off like a pair of rutting bulls.'

The teamster was not very concerned in that. 'What the hell are we settin' here for? How much farther to the town?'

'Two, three miles. But Fanning and them boys with him is upset about the captives in your wagon, an' their connection with the army.'

The teamster leaned aside to expectorate before speaking again. 'Well; we goin' to set out here all day? Nothing to be done about them captives. All I want is to get rid of this contraband cargo and get the hell out of this country.'

Charley Skinner's attitude stiffened noticeably when he said, 'We wait until Ira tells you otherwise, and seemed to me back yonder where Ira hired your outfit you was willing enough to run a little contraband.'

Skinner went back toward the head of the train and the teamster turned on his seat and swore. 'Nice mess you two got us into.'

Al Whitten's rebuttal was blunt and short. 'We didn't get you into anything, mister, you got yourself into it.'

Further discussion was cut short when someone up ahead called for the wagons to roll and the teamster sat forward with lines in both hands.

Crowfoot, who had spent most of this halt with his flour sack, got comfortable again. As the wagon moved he jutted his head toward a ratchet-jack roped against the far side of their wagon back near the tailgate.

Without making clear whatever he had in mind, Crowfoot began tumbling and snake-crawling as best he could wearing chains until he was near the jack handle, which was straight out from its tethered base and about four inches off the wagon bed.

When he began manoeuvering it dawned on Alan Whitten what he had thought of, and was now trying to implement: Get his clevis bolt over the jack handle.

Some men calling back and forth outside caused Crowfoot to stop writhing and listen. It sounded like some of the townsmen were leaving, heading east in the direction of Burnt Timbers.

After they had gone and while the teamster was glumly hunched on his seat, a leathery-faced, gaunt man swung up and said, 'Curtis, there's some kind of jangle over the guns. Them fellers who was just there didn't want them brought to Burnt Timbers.'

Al Whitten alternately watched Tom Crowfoot and the hunched men on the wagon seat out front.

The teamster's angry loud voice held Whitten's interest forward. 'Well now, by gawd I hauled their freight in good faith for darn near a hunnert miles, they've worn down my animals and now we're not goin' to be allowed in Burnt Timbers. Well, let me tell you something, Otis. Whether we dump the guns an' crates right out here in plain sight, or deliver them to that damned town, Ira's still goin' to pay me. It's not my fault ...'

'Hold it,' the dark-hided man said. 'Wasn't no mention of anyone not gettin' paid, and Ira told that Fanning feller we're goin' to deliver these guns come hell or high water ... Curtis, I don't like none of this. Ira'n Charley are sure the army's somewhere behind us. Ain't no sign yet an' Charley is goin' back to watch, but the way this looks to me is that us hired teamsters is goin' to get caught between a rock an' a hard place – with contraband in our wagons – and if it ain't the army it'll be someone else. You see what I'm drivin' at?'

Evidently Curtis saw, because he sat forward looking bitterly at his horse as he said, 'Somethin' you don't know, Otis. Them guns and the ammunition for 'em was stole from an army depot over east of here at a place called Fort A.P. Hill.'

Whitten heard the leathery-skinned man gasp. 'You sure of that, Curtis?'

'I'm sure of it.'

'Why'n hell didn't you let the rest of us know?'

Curtis turned a glum look on his companion. 'You'd have hired on anyway.'

'Like hell I …'

'Otis, I've known you close to fifteen years. In that time I've heard all the rumours of what you've hauled, an' most of it ain't any different from what you're hauling now, so don't go gettin' righteous on me.'

Otis was silent for a long time, but eventually he said, 'Does Ira know them guns was stolen?'

'Of course he knows. He put this whole damned thing together, didn't he?'

Again Otis was silent for a while before speaking. 'Well, I didn't know an' as far as I know none of the other teamsters knew, an' they aren't goin' to like it.'

Evidently Curtis was tired of this conversation because his reply was blunt. 'Know or not, you'n me an' the others hauled 'em, and every blessed one of us knew Gatling guns are army property an' haulin' them except for the army can get our necks pretty close to a hangrope.'

Otis jumped down from the wagon and walked ahead. His wagon was fifth in line, Curtis's wagon was the last one in the line.

Tom Crowfoot caught Whitten's eye and smiled, moved slowly and brought both hands around in front. The chains were not on them. He had successfuly got the jack-handle inside the clevis bolt and had jockeyed around until he had worked the bolt loose.

He was sweating and grinned wolfishly as he worked his way forward, stopped opposite Whitten and said, 'Lean forward.'

As Al started to lean the teamster twisted to look back. Al straightened back and Tom Crowfoot put both hands behind his back. Maybe someone else would have wondered but the teamster was burdened with his own problem as he said, 'You fellers hear any of that?'

Crowfoot hadn't but Whitten had. He nodded and asked a question. 'I thought this was a community affair. The way it sounded to me ...'

'An' now you know different, don't you?' growled the teamster. 'We worked our butts off, wore down our livestock, tried to avoid everyone – and then we got hooked into deliverin' two wagons to your fort, an' from there on everything come unravelled.'

'This whole idea came from those cowmen?'

'You didn't have to be real smart to figure that out,' Curtis snapped. 'They got money. When they banded together it come to quite a respectable amount of money. We're supposed to get paid twice our normal freighting rate, otherwise you'd never have caught me haulin' contraband so damned far.'

Al Whitten rattled his chains as he moved a little before speaking. 'What about the cowmen? Are they goin' to help you deliver the guns?'

'How the hell do I know? Ira sets up there in the lead wagon hardly more'n passin' the time of the day with us when we stop.'

'Why did they want to take the guns into the town up yonder?'

Curtis rolled his eyes. 'Because couple of them cowmen own buildings there. One's got a warehouse. That's where we're supposed to unload – after dark.'

'Who were those other fellers?'

Curtis grimaced. 'Townsmen. I got no idea how they knew, but I've lived long enough to know if you want to keep a secret, be the first to tell it. Hell, eight or ten ranchers connivin' together ... Somethin' like this just naturally gets out. If I'd known back ...'

Charley Skinner rode by, and paused on his way to scout down their trail to say, 'Ira says to keep going until you got the town in sight, then he'll tell you what to do next.'

Curtis sourly watched Skinner lope down their back trail and groaned aloud. 'He's so damned clever, him and Ira. It'll be an easy haul they said an' no danger.'

Al Whitten brushed past the grumbling to say, 'The army can't be too far back.'

Curtis did not even act like he'd heard. The longer he dwelt upon their dilemma the worse he felt, not only disgusted but threatened.

Someone in one of the forward wagons sang out. Curtis leaned to the far side of his seat and shaded his eyes. There were rooftops in the distance. Burnt Timbers was a lot larger than the last time he'd seen it. Back then it had been just another starve-out settler village.

The day had been wearing along; it would still be quite a while before dark, but shadows were beginning to appear on the lee side of brush and boulders.

Al Whitten and Tom Crowfoot took full advantage of the teamster's interest in the town up ahead. Tom had the jack-handle. He inserted it into the clevis bolt, exerted strong pressure, then tapped the bolt-head and un-screwed it as easily as though it had never been tightened.

Al shed his chains as quietly as he could and, like Crowfoot, left the ones around his ankles lying there in plain sight. Whitten's heart was pounding. They were free; at least they were no longer chained.

Curtis spoke casually as he straightened back to correct the slight drift of his horses. 'Maybe they got it settled. There's no one up yonder to block our way.'

Whitten and Crowfoot exchanged a look; when a man looked for encouragement he could always find it, irra-tional though it might be. Maybe the wagon train's dilemma would be resolved handily, but after what Curtis had said it seemed to both of them this would not be.

They stopped again. This time Curtis looped his lines, set his binders and went down the side of his wagon like a spider after a fly. Whitten said, 'Mad as a hornet.'

Crowfoot was not interested in Curtis's mood. He pushed the chains off his lower legs and was leaning to arise when a loud argument erupted near the tailgate. One of the raised voices belonged to their teamster, the other voice belonged to the other large man with the wagons: Ira Blakely.

'You start an' stop like a backin' an' fillin' colt, Ira. Are we goin' into that damned town or aren't we?'

For one moment Ira's voice was calm. But only for a moment. The other man's explosion had caught him unprepared. 'Of course we're goin' over there like we planned, but first them ranchers got to scout up the place ... An' who the hell do you think you are, questionin' me! You just drive your wagon and do what I tell you!'

For two seconds there was not a sound, then, when it came, it wasn't words, it was the solid meeting of bone against bone.

From nearby several men squawked at once and began running toward Curtis's tailgate, but before they arrived whoever had been struck roared a curse and attacked.

Whitten and Crowfoot could not resist, they crept to the tailgate and hoisted the canvas a fraction. Big Ira Blakely and Curtis were toe to toe slugging it out. Once in a while one or the other would take a hard hit and grunt, but neither would yield ground.

The onlookers halted well out of the way. Some yelled for the fighting to stop. Others rooted for one fighter or the other. To Al Whitten it seemed, since both battlers were equal in heft and solidness, sooner or later someone was going to land a lucky blow.

But that is not how it ended. That skinny teamster named Otis fired his handgun into the ground between the battlers. The gout of exploding earth as much as the thunderous report of the gun caught and momentarily held everyone's attention. Otis said, 'We got enough trouble 'thout you two makin' more. Now that's enough … Curtis, get back on your seat. Ira, explain right now what the hell we're supposed to do!'

Curtis did not leave, but stood wide-legged, breathing hard and glaring at the wagon boss. Ira, however, had perhaps been worrying after he'd been hurt a couple of times, and this opportunity was all he needed. He picked up his hat, pushed it atop his head and ignored Curtis to adress Otis and the others.

'Them cowmen rode to town. They're going to muzzle them townsmen who came out here. We're to set still until dark then drive into town along the back of the place on the east side.'

Curtis sarcastically said, 'How'll we know it's safe to go over there?'

Ira turned slowly. 'Because one of 'em'll ride back an' guide us in.' He continued to glare at Curtis and would have said something else, but an older freighter with thin hair and perpetually narrowed eyes spoke first. He had a gruff, harsh voice. 'I tell you, what, Ira. This'll be the last time I hire out to you.' He turned and stalked in the direction of his wagon.

Whitten and Crowfoot were back up front with chains draped over their ankles by the time Curtis climbed back to his seat and looked behind it. Shadows were thickening, evening was on the way, the inside of a wagon with a canvas top got darker faster than the outside did. Curtis leaned on the back of his seat and squinted.

Crowfoot said, 'What was the fight about?'

Curtis glared at the 'breed. 'You deef? It wasn't ten, fifteen feet from the tailgate … I'm fed up with Ira blunderin' from one stupid mistake into another one. At the rate he's bossin' things the damned army'll be around us come sunrise.'

Tom Crowfoot nodded about that, and faintly smiled,

but visibility down inside the wagon was not good enough for Curtis to notice that. Alan Whitten did not see the faint smile either.

Curtis rummaged in his 'possible' box on the far side of the wagon, fished out a tin of salve and sat dourly massaging salve into his hands. He hadn't been hurt, but his fists were as sore as boils.

As he put the tin back and slammed the lid on his 'possible' box he straightened around, studied the distant town, visible now only as a covey of wavery lights, and leaned over the back of his seat again as he said, 'I'm goin' to grain the horses,' and began climbing into the back of his wagon toward the grain barrel.

Whitten had little time to be startled. Neither did Tom Crowfoot, but when Curtis brushed against the chain on Whitten's ankles it fell away. Curtis had only a moment to be surprised before Tom shoved the jack-handle into his back and said, 'You so much as wheeze an' I'll run this knife clean through you.'

Curtis, stooped slightly, remained fixed in that position as they emptied his holster, went over him for a hide-out, found a wicked-bladed boot knife and took that too. Not a word had been said since Crowfoot's first threat. Curtis was dumbfounded. If they'd been tied with rope he would have had less difficulty accepting the situation, but they had been chained.

They pushed him to the floorboards. Whitten had his sixgun, the 'breed had his big knife, and if Whitten did not look particularly menacing the 'breed certainly did. He grinned from ear to ear and held the flat part of the knife to Curtis's throat as he said, 'Just keep your voice down.'

Curtis had no trouble obeying, he hadn't made a sound since his capture and did not make any now as he stared from one of them to the other.

Tom Crowfoot finally eased back a little with the knife, as he said, 'Army'll be along directly. Does Ira figure to use them two guns that are primed and ready?'

Curtis raised his lowered shoulders. 'I wouldn't bet he wouldn't use 'em, but I just plain don't know ... He's crazy enough to. There was talk a while back of masscreein' the soldiers and blamin' it on the In'ians.'

Al Whitten had a question. 'Which wagons got those two loaded guns?'

'The wagon directly in front of us, and the wagon Ira's ridin' in.' Curtis had found his voice. 'Wait a minute: You two got loose. Don't waste no time hangin' around. Get the hell away from here as fast as you can run.'

Al Whitten stood up, had to slump a little to avoid contact with the canvas top, and Tom Crowfoot grinned at the teamster. 'You gave us water an' made Skinner fetch some jerky. Curtis, if you want to stay alive you better leave your rig an' come with us.'

'Leave my wagon an' horses? Not on your damned life. I'll take my chances.'

Crowfoot leaned with the knife-point inches from Curtis's breastbone. 'I was being kindly,' he said, and pushed the blade until it was against cloth. 'We can't leave you behind.'

Curtis snorted. 'You think, when the order comes to roll, an' my rig don't move, they won't come back here, see them empty chains and guess what happened?'

Crowfoot pushed a half inch and blood appeared from the tiny scratch. He jerked his head. 'Look out front, If there's no one around, let us know an' all three of us'll leave. *Get up!*'

# SIX
# A Long Night

Except for descending darkness they probably would have been unable to leave the train. Curtis had performed one helpful act from outside his rig; he eased off the binders, slackened the lines of his hitch, and horses being horses, when the wagon up ahead, tooled by that leathery-skinned man named Otis, moved out, Curtis's animals with no restraining hand would follow out of the habit they'd formed since the Blakely train had first left some settlements many miles eastward.

But he was not happy to leave. Those horses and that wagon, along with his gatherings inside it, were all he owned in this world.

With Tom Crowfoot leading they made it safely to a shallow arroyo and halted there to watch the dark shape of a horseman arrive up near the front wagon, after which within a few minutes, Ira gave the whistle which started the wagons moving again.

Curtis watched his wordly possessions dutifully following Otis's wagon and sadly wagged his head. Whitten said, 'Better'n gettin' your butt in a wringer, an' you'll get it all back anyway.'

Curtis put a dark scowl on Alan Whitten. 'You're sure of that, are you?'

Tom Crowfoot stood up as the last wagon faded in the direction of Burnt Timbers, listened to the night before

59

hunkering down to say, 'Al ...?'

Since being freed Whitten had been toying with several notions and only one of them made much sense – await the arrival of the patrol. The others were dangerous. One of them was almost suicidal: Get to the wagons, set one afire and hope they could get away before firelight limned them. He started to mention this and before he'd got the idea half stated Curtis grabbed a handful of Alan's shirt and said, 'You'll blow up the animals. What'd they do?' He released his grip and shoved Alan back a little. 'And burn the wagons, including mine. Not on your damned life, mister!'

'All right. In the dark we can shag them on foot,' Whitten suggested. 'Maybe get into the town an' find those fellers who are against what those cowmen got in mind.'

Curtis still scowled but at least this time he offered no argument. But Tom Crowfoot did. He said, 'All we got to do is set an' wait.'

Curtis growled. 'For what?'

'The army,' Tom replied and Whitten snapped at him. 'You know what Skinner did, tied our horses in tandem so's the patrol will take the wrong trail.'

Tom Crowfoot grinned in the gloom. 'All right, we can stalk the town but it's goin' to be a lot of walkin' we wouldn't have to do if we just waited.'

Curtis glowered at Crowfoot. 'How long? They'll most likely have them guns and shell boxes unloaded and be away from there before dawn.' He shrugged mighty shoulders and held out his hand toward Al Whitten. 'My pistol.'

Al handed it over as Tom gradually stiffened with his head to one side. He said nothing for a long time, and when he finally did speak he gestured with an upraised arm. 'I told you it wouldn't be long. What's that sound like to you, Al?'

Whitten listened, faintly frowned and said, 'Horses in

line, but it can't be, Tom. Before sundown they'd have found that false trail. They'll be five miles away an' still ridin' in the wrong direction.'

Tom Crowfoot arose, stood with his head cocked for a moment then brushed Whitten's shoulder with his fingers. 'Stay here. I'm goin' to find him.'

Crowfoot faded into the night without a sound and the burly teamster scowled as he said, 'Find who? ... Is he crazy? Them 'breeds is ...'

'Yeah he's crazy, mister. He's so crazy he's one of the best scouts in the country. We're not goin' anywhere anyway.'

That reply did not satisfy the burly teamster but he sat back listening to diminishing sounds of wagons, one of which was his own. He also gently massaged his slightly swollen knuckles, which Al watched him do for a while, until they both heard a night bird make its mournful call, and get an answer after a short interval, then the teamster's eyes narrowed as his peered in the direction Tom Crowfoot had taken.

He grumbled. 'Damned tomahawks; your friend's likely run onto a band of his friends an' they'll come back an' lift our hair, or something.'

Al Whitten ignored the teamster. That night bird call was one of the first mimicking sounds he'd learned. It was not only common it was also a signal.

He eased back against the crumbly eastern side of their arroyo and concentrated on the darkness to his left while Curtis finished massaging his sore knuckles and was again straining to hear the wagons. He grunted, finally, and turned toward Whitten with his mouth open to speak. It remained open but no sound came out. His eyes were round and his nostrils flared.

There were two of them on the west side of the arroyo. The one Curtis saw first was very dark, a little less than average height, with straight, coarse black hair and a long-barreled sixgun dangling at his right side.

Curtis's breath jammed in his chest. This was Apache country, night or day made no difference. Curtis had his holstered Colt but that very dark bronco already had his weapon in his fist.

A quiet voice spoke from slightly behind and south of the dark Indian. 'Told you they'd be along, all we had to do was wait.'

Curtis watched Tom Crowfoot and the dark Indian who had startled the whey out of him come down into the arroyo and squat near Whitten. None of those three heeded the teamster as they exchanged sentences that sounded like bursts of gibberish.

Whitten finally faced the teamster. 'The patrol's out there waitin' for this feller, Everett Tanyard, to return.'

Curtis glowered. Indians made him uncomfortable and always had, but tonight this particular dark bronco troubled him more than he would have admitted.

He ignored the Indians to ask how soldiers had got up so close so fast, when Charley Skinner had bragged of making a very clever ruse so's they'd take the wrong trail.

Everett Tanyard, who was not at all dense despite a customary expressionless look, addressed the teamster for the first time. He jutted his jaw Indian fashion in Tom's direction. 'You know him?'

'Well; we met. What about him?'

'You know his name?'

'The other scout called him Crowfoot.'

Whitten and the pair of 'breeds grinned widely at the teamster, sharing a secret until Everett Tanyard leaned in the night gloom and with a rigid finger made the imprint of a crow's four-toed foot in arroyo dust.

Curtis squinted and scowled but said nothing.

Everett Tanyard repeated the sign-painting, this time with the foremost toe and the one on each side pointing in the direction the wagons had taken. He straightened back waiting for the teamster to understand. Instead, Curtis glared. 'I ain't in no mood for games, In'ian.'

Crowfoot said, 'Look; that crow track is pointing where the wagons went.'

'I ain't blind. He already ...'

'Shut up,' Crowfoot snapped and pointed to the crow foot sign. 'Since about sundown last night I been leavin' a crowfoot sign in white flour from a sack in your wagon. Got a fistful of flour and each time we stopped I shoved my fist through a hole in the floor of your wagon and used my fingers an' wrist to make an outline of a crow's foot pointin' in the way the wagons was taking ... Not for the wagons, mister; I didn't give a damn about the wagons. I left that sign for someone from the fort to see and know what it meant: Crowfoot's in one of the wagons goin' in the direction of the sign.'

Tanyard added a little more, perhaps as much for the benefit of Al Whitten as for the teamster's enlightenment. 'We saw where two saddlehorses had gone north side by side.'

'And ...?'

Tanyard made one of his rare smiles. 'An' mister, I'd already seen the first of them white crowfoot signs. White as snow, an' kept on that trail. The captain detached a feller to find them horses and bring 'em along, with instructions that if he run into trouble to fire off a round and we'd all turn back for him.'

Tanyard's smile was fading. 'There wasn't no shot. I never expected there would be. I led off in a lope for a couple miles, seen more of Crowfoot's sign, an' here we are, mister ... An' we watched them wagons head for that settlement.' Tanyard looked from Crowfoot to Whitten. He had already been told what was in the wagons.

The teamster sat a long moment contemplating a particularly bright star, then spat and stood up. The sound of wagons was faint, none of them were visible. He looked southward, but there was neither sound nor movement in that direction.

Everett Tanyard went to his horse, snugged up the cinch preparatory to mounting, and said, 'I'll bring 'em up. You fellers set easy.'

Curtis watched Everett Tanyard until he was lost in nightgloom, then he sank down again, silent but with busy thoughts.

Al Whitten shoved back his hat and got comfortable as he gazed irritably at Tom Crowfoot. 'I knew you were doin' somethin' back there with that flour sack.'

Tom grinned, crossed his legs and plucked a nearby dry grass stalk to chew.

Curtis had been wrestling with his particular problem. It was fairly simple: He had been hauling contraband, and Army courts were not like civilian courts. For one thing an army court required 'specifications' and charges, civilian courts required evidence pro and con. They also required lawyers for the prosecution and for the defence. Military courts were not notorious for their lenience: In cases of capital crimes such as murder, military courts offered a choice between a firing squad or a hanging. In cases involving hauling contraband, especially stolen contraband, violaters had been shot. If spared the firing squad they were very likely to be sentenced to forty years in prison. There was no appeal, and military courts did not procrastinate: Whatever a culprit's sentence it was usually carried out within three or four days.

Curtis finally addressed Al Whitten. 'Them guns was stolen,' he said. Whitten nodded because he had already heard Curtis say this to the teamster named Otis.

'Them cowmen pooled a lot of money to buy 'em. To bring over here to ….'

'And you helped steal them, Curtis?'

The teamster bristled. 'No by gawd. Me'n some other fellers met some flatbed wagons at night. As soon as I saw what Blakely had contracted to haul, I wasn't the only feller who squawked. Ira offered us more money'd we make in six months of regular hauling.'

'But you knew the guns and ammunition had been stolen?'

Curtis got a pained look on his face. 'I never asked an' Ira never told me.'

'Then how did you know?'

'How else could Ira have got hold of Gatlin' guns? You can't order them through a catalogue an' I've yet to see one on display in a store. Of course they was stolen. An' I'd guess that by now where Ira stoled them from some army depot there's hell bein' raised and propped up ... But that's not what bothers me. Ira's in trouble up to his gullet. The rest of us hired on to make a haul for him ... But who'd believe us if we said we didn't know what them guns was in our wagons, or that it's against the law to own them unless you're in the army, an' even then you can operate 'em but you can't own one?'

Whitten eyed the burly teamster and said nothing. There was actually nothing to be said. The Gatling guns had been stolen from the army, Curtis had hauled them and now the army was coming up, and when it found those guns, heard how they had reached Burnt Timbers, Ira Blakely would indeed be in trouble up to his gullet, but so would Curtis, Otis, and the other teamsters, as well as their hired swampers.

None of this was Al Whitten's immediate concern. He was sitting there in the warm night, waiting for those whose authority in the Territory made it *their* concern.

Tom snored, which attracted the attention of his companions in the arroyo. Curtis sniffed, "Breeds ain't got sense enough to be worried.'

Whitten replied to that sharply. 'They usually don't have no reason; they do what they get paid for an' don't get involved in contraband ... Maybe a hide-out bottle of whiskey now'n then, but that's all.'

Curtis seemed to ignore the retort. He was massaging his knuckles again, and was still doing it when the distinct sound of riders approaching from the south became audible, then he stopped the massaging and raised a haggard face.

He was armed, but he stood about as much chance of using a weapon to get clear as a snowball in hell. He sighed, wagged his head and slowly arose to his full height.

Whitten shook Crowfoot awake. They both also stood up. A pair of horsemen emerged from the night; Everett Tanyard and Captain Herbert Morris. They stopped upon the lip of the arroyo and sat with hands atop their saddle-bows. Both rode regulation McClellen saddles which had no horns.

Captain Morris removed his gauntlets without haste and folded them under and over his garrison belt. He leaned to push the metal scabbard of his saber back so that it would not interfere as he dismounted, and looked a long time at Curtis. After swinging to the ground he asked the teamster's name.

'Curtis Glidden.'

'Where are the Gatling guns, Mister Glidden?'

Curtis pointed with an oaken arm. 'Pretty close to Burnt Timbers by now.'

The captain cocked an eyebrow at Al Whitten, who explained how he and Tom Crowfoot had been caught and how they had escaped taking the burly teamster with them.

Captain Morris gazed from Whitten to Crowfoot. The impression was that he wanted to give them a sound tongue lashing, but he instead sighed, spat aside, tugged forth his gauntlets and was pulling them on when a red-faced veteran sergeant came up with the rest of the patrol.

Al counted and raised his eyes. Patrols ordinarily consisted of from ten to fifteen men. Captain Morris's patrol had thirty men in it. Darn near company size.

Morris saw Whitten's expression and loosened a little. 'Well, I didn't think you and Tom went joy-riding. You had something in mind, and it just about had to do with those wagons.' The captain turned as the red-headed sergeant came up, halted, and stared from the scouts to the burly freighter.

Captain Morris said, 'Tell you later. Right now we got to mount up Whitten an' Crowfoot. Who's got their horses back yonder?'

Two troopers came up leading led horses. They impassively tossed the reins to the scouts and turned back to their position near the end of the detail.

The veteran sergeant jutted his jaw. 'What about him?' he asked and the captain gazed stonily at the teamster. 'He's goin' to walk until we come onto something he can ride. Al, you'n Tom an' Everett scout ahead. How far to that village?'

Crowfoot replied, 'Two, three miles, an' my guess is that by now everyone over there is wide awake. Some of the townsmen don't want no Gatling guns in their town.'

Captain Morris was leading off when he asked Al Whitten what in tarnation anyone wanted with Gatling guns out here, anyway.

Alan explained and the men who heard him, and who had not heard the story before, were solemnly silent. Not because they were particularly averse to having the savage raghead Apaches whipped to a frazzle, but because they were shocked at what local stockmen had banded together to do, which would simply be a wholesale massacre.

It wasn't fighting Indians that bothered them, it was the way the rangemen intended to do it. There would be no Apaches left if the stockmen got their Gatling guns positioned on the rims overlooking Apache canyon.

The grizzled sergeant spat out a cud of tobacco, exchanged a look with Al Whitten and shook his head without saying a word.

Captain Morris made a dry statement which broke a long silence broken only by the sound of horses and their equipment rattling and rubbing.

'How many stockmen will we be dealing with, Mister Glidden?'

Curtis looked surprised. 'I got no idea, Captain. Near as I figured from the ones come out to the train … maybe thirty.'

'How many men in town who favour their scheme; you got any idea?'

'No sir. None at all.'

'But there are townsmen who are against it?'

'Well, they're against havin' them Gatlin' guns kept in town … My guess it that they're scairt someone who knows they're in Burnt Timbers might go runnin' to the army.'

Captain Morris said no more, he sat straight up in the saddle eyeing lights up ahead through the darkness. When he'd completed his study he asked if anyone knew how many people lived over there.

Curtis Glidden waited; when no one spoke he offered an answer. 'Four, five hunnert. I was over there last fall. The place had grown considerable since the other time I was over there … five, six years back.'

The captain asked if there was a lawman. Curtis nodded about that. 'Stringbean of a feller named Perry Foreman, unless he's been replaced since last fall. I heard he was a cowboy who was appointed to the job by Burnt Timbers' town council.'

The captain raised a gauntleted hand to halt the column when they could all hear noise up ahead. There were also lamps, some stationary, others swinging as though men were carrying them.

Curtis bleakly said, 'Unloading. There's some ware-houses up there where we was to off-load the guns and the ammunition.'

Captain Morris waited until the scouts came back, listened to their reports, and dismounted to stand beside his horse for a long time lost in thought.

# SEVEN
# A Very Bright Night

The lights at Burnt Timbers seemed to be mostly at the upper, or north, end of town. There were lights elsewhere but less noticeable and not numerous. The town was awake, but was either not as fully aroused, or as interested, as it might have been had those wagons arrived in daylight.

The captain jerked his head for Alan Whitten to come up, and when he approached the officer said, 'Scout, Alan.'

Whitten nodded. 'I'll take Tom and ...'

'You go alone. Stay clear but look and listen.'

As Whitten went back for his horse and Tom Crowfoot would have cinched up Alan shook his head. 'I'm to go alone.'

Tom stood watching Whitten ride at a walk toward the distant town. Behind him a leg-weary teamster said, 'Better to lose one than both of you. They know you fellers escaped.' Curtis paused watching the shifting distant lights. 'If they get him this time they'll bust his skull. Specially Ira or Charley Skinner.'

None of the men who heard the teamster either looked at him or commented. The officer came down among the dismounted men standing at the heads of their horses, sought out the red-headed sergeant and spoke quietly. 'We should send someone back. Major

69

Burroughs wouldn't like it, us storming in over there with maybe as many men as we got against us, and gawd knows about the town.'

The old campaigner replied while watching those yonder lights. 'For a fact he wouldn't like it, Captain, but if we wait until he gets here with the rest of the garrison them guns'll be unloaded an' maybe on their way to the rims above Apache Canyon, an' if they get there first, he'll like what'll happen a hell of a lot less … Specially when he's got to make his report of what happened, and how come his command let it happen.'

Captain Morris also faced toward the distant lights. It was his decision, and his alone. Eventually he said, 'All right; stand to horse until Whitten gets back,' and walked back up near the front of the troop where Tom Crowfoot and the unhappy teamster were squatting in desultory conversation, which they terminated when the officer appeared.

Everett Tanyard was squatting too, but he was adding nothing to the discussion and occasionally when Curtis looked at him, the hair on the back of his neck stood erect. Everett was one of those 'breeds who aroused bad feelings in most whiteskins just by his presence and long silences.

A trooper sputtered a sulphur match to life to fire up a quirley and half the column came down on him. The flare died underfoot and the uncomplimentary comments continued nearly as long as did the pungent odour of the match.

The veteran sergeant said, 'Recruits! May gawd deliver me from recruits!'

Whitten did not return for about an hour. He had made a thorough scout. When he swung to the ground near Captain Morris he said, 'They got the guns unloaded an' inside a big old log building. They're unloading the ammunition boxes now, an' there's a lot more rangemen than was with the wagons earlier; looked to me like there might be maybe forty or fifty.'

'Townsmen, Alan?'

'Well; they're over there, but don't seem willing to do much, an' a man can't blame them.'

'How many?'

Alan shrugged. 'I'd guess maybe twenty, mostly staying clear of the log barn where the ammunition is bein' unloaded.' Alan turned to look back. 'It's up to you, Captain. We can come in from the north an' south, get on both sides of that log warehouse, or whatever it is.' He faced around slowly. 'It may not amount to much if there's a fight.'

Curtis, Tom and Everett had ambled up to listen. The teamster said, 'It'll be a fight, gents, don't fool yourselves about that. Them stockmen who come out to ride with the wagons had their backs up.'

Captain Morris stood with thumbs hooked in his garrison belt watching the lights. His ultimate decision surprised those closest to him. 'We'll wait until everything is unloaded ... Mister Glidden, do the teamsters aim to bed down over there?'

'Most likely, Captain. They'll be tired enough, an' there's the matter of gettin' paid, which Ira said wouldn't happen until we'd delivered and off-loaded the cargo.'

Captain Morris was silent again for a long moment, facing the village. He finally addressed the scouts. 'We'll wait until the town's quiet, folks are bedded down, then we'll slip over there on foot and fire that damned warehouse.'

Not a word was said. In fact the silence was so deep when a horse whinnied back down the trail it sounded very loud, and Al Whitten's reaction startled everyone.

'Son of a bitch! Tom ... Skinner sure as hell; he went scoutin' down the back trail!'

Crowfoot stared into the darkness where the horse had made its racket. 'If it was,' he eventually said, 'then he knows we're out here.'

That question was settled when they heard the sound of a running horse heading on a northwesterly angle from somewhere behind the column in the direction of the village.

Explanations were required so Alan Whitten offered them. When he finished talking Captain Morris shifted weight from one leg to the other one, was silent a long time and concentrated on the village.

The teamster put everyone's thoughts into perspective when he said, 'So much for sneakin' up over there. Charley'll set the fox among the chickens. Ira'll have somethin' to worry about he wasn't expecting after Charley told him how clever he'd been settin' a false trail.' He swung his head toward Tom Crowfoot. 'You'n your damned flour sack!'

Everett Tanyard entered the discussion for the first time, speaking in a gruff voice. 'I can get up to that place where they got the ammunition an' guns.'

Even Captain Morris stared at him. Curtis replied sourly. 'Not unless you can make yourself invisible. They'll have armed sentinels thick as hair on a dog's back.'

Everett was adamant. 'I can get up there.'

Silence followed; Whitten and Crowfoot thought it likely that Tanyard could do it. They were also convinced that it would take a lot of time for him to get over there and neither of them had much of an idea how much darkness would be left.

Captain Morris looked from Tanyard to Crowfoot and Alan Whitten. 'One might make it out of three,' he murmured.

Al was ready, he handed his carbine to a trooper and waited until the pair of 'breeds had done the same, then he nodded to the captain and would have walked away but the officer said, 'Wait,' and called up the veteran sergeant. 'Any dynamite?' he asked, and got a negative shake of the sergeant's head, accompanied by an old campaigner's suggestion. 'We can make up a couple of pouches of gunpowder, that ought to work. I've seen it done.'

Captain Morris nodded at the sergeant and as the old campaigner went among the dismounted troopers the captain smiled without a shred of humour.

While they waited the teamster wagged his head. He'd heard some crazy ideas in his time but this had to be about the craziest. 'If they get up there, sure as hell they'll never get back.'

No one took that up, but Captain Morris gazed dispassionately at the burly man for a moment, then turned away.

It was the grizzled sergeant, as old as the teamster and only slightly less thick, who tapped the burly man's shoulder as he said, 'You got a better idea?'

'No. I got no idea at ....'

'Then shut your damned mouth an' keep it shut!'

Curtis was not an individual who accepted that kind of talk, but every man close enough to have heard the exchange was looking steadily at him. If he made a move toward the sergeant he was very likely going to get clubbed by a dozen troopers. Curtis fished in a pocket for his cut plug and ignored the others as he tore off a corner and tucked the cud into his cheek.

As the sergeant handed three small bundles to the captain he volunteered to go with the scouts. Captain Morris shook his head without speaking, handed the little bundles to Al Whitten and made a hard little smile. 'Good luck.'

Within moments the scout disappeared in darkness and behind them the captain told his men to loosen their cinches and get comfortable. He anticipated a long wait.

Two of his contingent looked in the direction of the eastern horizon. One was the sergeant, the other was Curtis Glidden, the disgruntled teamster.

Al kept Crowfoot and Tanyard with him until they

were less than half a mile from the village. There, they
squatted and watched lights.

If Ira Blakely had taken heed of his scout's report
there seemed to be no sign of it. None of the activity up
yonder seemed different from what it had been. In fact
there appeared finally to be fewer lights, mostly at the
lower end of town. Crowfoot said, 'Townsmen give up
an' gone back to bed.'

It was a reasonable notion but Al remained in place
for a long time without agreeing or disagreeing. When
he finally grunted and led off he handed each of the
'breeds one of the little pouches of gunpowder and also
gave each man several sulphur matches.

What he had been wondering about during their time
of sitting and watching, was whether or not a townsman
might take it on himself to try and ride away from the
village. It seemed reasonable if there was as much
opposition to what the stockmen were up to as seemed
to be the case.

They moved without a sound, advancing in a low
crouch so as not to be skylined; darkness or not,
movement of any kind caught attention.

They were close enough to hear someone swearing at
some horses when Everett dropped flat. Whitten and
Crowfoot followed Tanyard's example. For a while
there was nothing to see, but eventually Everett reached
to gently brush Whitten's sleeve and jut his jaw.

Finally, Al and Tom saw the movement. A man was
crossing from north to south in front of them about two
hundred feet, which was nearly the extent of visibility.
He had a Winchester in the crook of one arm.

They watched him. Al speculated about his purpose.
If Blakely'd put scouts out with orders to constantly
patrol, getting past would be more difficult than if the
guards were stationary.

He was beginning to believe reaching their goal this
time was going to be much more difficult than getting

inside that wagon had been back where they'd been caught.

He felt like swearing; if Skinner had not come onto the soldiers on his ride back from the back-trail the chance of getting up to the storehouse would have been much simpler.

Tom leaned to whisper. 'He met another feller down south. Looks like they're talking.'

Tanyard said, 'Like soldiers; they patrol one way until they meet another feller, then patrol back the way they come. Wait.'

They waited and exactly as Everett had predicted, the patrolling man with the gun in the crook of his arm came striding back. He did not look left nor right, which would not have mattered because the three scouts were belly-down in tall grass.

Up ahead where there were fewer lights, someone called. Whatever that signified none of the scouts had any idea. It would have been better if they'd had some notion, because Charley Skinner had called to the nearest patrolling sentry that he was coming through to scout up the soldiers.

A barking dog had his excited noise stopped in mid-bark, and yelped once before becoming silent.

There was almost no noise coming from the village as the scouts waited for their strolling sentry to pass southward again. As soon as he was out of sight they spread out a little and belly-crawled to within a yard or so of the route he would use on his return.

They probably could have slithered past before he came back, but it was not a chance Whitten wanted to take. They were as still as lizards as the man returned, walking without haste nor much interest in what he was doing. He probably never felt the rough stag handle of the knife Everett Tanyard struck him in the back of the head with.

He was lying face up when Whitten and Crowfoot

passed. Both recognised him at the same time; Otis, the leathery-hided thin man who had tooled the wagon in front of Curtis's outfit.

This action assured the need for haste. Sooner or later someone would find Otis.

They ran crouched when they dared and belly-crawled when being upright was too dangerous. In this way they reached the vicinity of the log warehouse, and here the sentries were closer together, too close in fact for anyone to get near enough to fire the structure.

Whitten, fearful of what was behind them, now that he was almost certain someone had found Otis, did not take time to study the habits of these stationary armed men. He looked for one that might be sitting with his back to the warehouse, as had happened back where they'd been caught, but if there were weary men up here, and undoubtedly there were, he saw no indication of it. Each guard had a Winchester as well as a sidearm.

He had a dry throat by the time he decided they could only set their fires by taking out one, perhaps two, of the guards, and as closely spaced as they all were, if one man was seen to fall by others nearby, hell would break loose.

All hell broke loose anyway.

Somewhere behind them, more distant than it seemed by the sound, a flurry of gunshots erupted. Immediately the armed guards became alert, and to the north a man's bull-bass bellow warned that the army was probably coming, a suggestion that inspired most of the guards to push eastward toward the sounds of earlier gunfire.

One guard halted no more than twenty feet from the stalkers in the grass, too far for them to knock him senseless before he could use his Winchester.

He was a lean man with a dark beard and a hooked nose. He was peering intently in the direction of that gunfire. Al Whitten knew the man would look down eventually, so he drew his handgun and cocked it. The guard did look down. He also stiffened in his boots but wisely made no move to aim or cock his Winchester.

Tom Crowfoot arose from the grass, swung his Colt barrel in a vicious, sharp arc which punched the stranger's hat down over his ears and knocked him senseless.

Al and Everett scurried past the downed guard, hesitated only a moment to peek around the south side of the log building, then to slip half away along and kneel to gather cured grass and leaves to start their separate fires with.

Al stood with his handgun ready but no one came down the side of the structure although there was noise of men running and calling behind the building.

As the flames brightened and snagged at cracks in the old dried logs of the building, Al led the flight southward keeping other buildings on his right to act as shelter.

He finally turned eastward, leaving cover behind, and ran with his Colt in a firm grip. Everett and Tom were close behind.

They got a fair distance eastward before someone in the darkness to their right challenged with a loud yell. Whitten took a chance and yelled back. 'They're in the village! Soldiers all over the place!'.

There was no reply but the challenger made distinctly audible sounds as he fled northward, not toward the village but northward behind it in the direction of perhaps a corral with horses in it.

Not until they heard men up ahead did the scouts drop flat again. This time it was those forward sentinels and they did not seem any less near panic than the guards back at the village. They had abandoned caution and were calling back and forth in the darkness, evidently wanting to gang together by following the sounds of the callers.

Only once did one of them yell something that interested the prone men in the tall grass: 'I told that crazy son of a bitch to leave everthin' an' run for it!'

The only reply he got was: 'Over here, Hank. Over where you hear me.'

They never saw 'Hank' or the man who had called directions to him. But they remained motionless and belly-down for as long as it seemed necessary before arising and starting east again, but this time in a trot instead of a run.

They still had no idea concerning that abrupt burst of gunfire, but somewhere ahead were the soldiers and their intention was to avoid getting shot at.

The last time they halted Whitten yelled ahead. For a while there was no response so he yelled again, saying who he was and who was with him.

The distinct, hard voice of Captain Morris telling his sergeant for the troopers to ground their arms made even Everett Tanyard smile.

They covered the last half mile at a tired walk. The first soldier they saw was that grizzled sergeant. He had walked out a short ways with a cocked pistol in his fist. When he saw them, recognised each one of them, he eased down the hammer, leathered his weapon and pointed.

They looked back. Burnt Timbers was as bright as day from the wild flames which were consuming the log warehouse. As the sergeant turned back with them he said, 'Any minute now.'

They found Captain Morris standing wide-legged and looking pleased. He was not smiling but as each scout came up he commended them individually, then pointed.

Every man with the column stared in awe at the raging fire. Evidently that big warehouse was old because its log walls could not have burned so hard and hot and fast if the wood han't been bone dry.

Whitten asked what the shooting had been about. The sergeant took him by the arm, walked down the line of soldiers who did not so much as glance at their passing, halted near a carelessly-flung blanket, stooped to lift it, and Al neither moved nor spoke until the sergeant dropped the blanket and said, 'He was sneakin' around. Couple of lads saw him, challenged him, an' when he run and fired, they riddled him. You know him?'

'Yeah. His name is Charley Skinner.'

The sergeant's eyes got round. 'By gawd, yes. I thought I recognised him. Well, his renegade trail is ended.'

# EIGHT
## More Surprises

Something that troubled the captain urged him to find Al Whitten and ask about starting the fire. As Alan explained what they had done there was a tremendous explosion. The ground shook underfoot and several troopers had trouble with their frightened horses.

In the direction of Burnt Timbers clearly visible firebrands were flying in all directions, the brilliance was as light as day and smoke-scent was punched in all directions by the force of the explosion.

The troopers watched in awe. It could be doubted that any of them had ever seen such a wild sight before, and most would perhaps never see its equal again.

Someone said, 'It'll take the whole town.'

There was no further comment. Echoes chased one another in all directions, the night had huge holes burned in it by flames leaping higher than any of the town's buildings.

It was possible to see running figures backgrounded by fire. It looked to Captain Morris as though a fire-brigade was being formed, but with all the noise, firelight and confusion he could have imagined that.

Everett and Tom Crowfoot came up where Whitten was standing, silent and awe-struck. Captain Morris moved away, back toward the head of the column where the grizzled sergeant said, 'We could ride in over there and grab us a corral full of stockmen.'

Morris did not even shake his head as he watched Burnt Timbers' conflagration and confusion. Clearly audible were screaming people. He replied to the sergeant in a dead-calm voice.

'Ride into that town right now, and they'd be as likely to start shooting at us as at anyone. Their town's being destroyed.'

The sergeant was matter-of-fact about that. 'Ain't the first time, Mister Morris. That's how it got its name. In'ians burnt it to the ground six, eight years back.'

A couple of soldiers bawled, almost in unison, and hauled their animals around to mount. The sergeant yelled at them and both troopers turned to stone, but one man called back to the sergeant. 'A rider's goin' past to the south.'

Captain Morris called to the soldiers. 'Go get him!'

Six troopers sprang over leather and disappeared in a flinging rush through the darkness.

There was another of those earth-shaking explosions. This time watchers clearly saw a heavy Gatling gun, wheels turning, rise up into the air, hang for a moment then go tumbling back into the maelstrom of nearly white flames.

The fire was spreading, and indeed a bucket brigade was furiously at work, but if it was having an effect it was not discernible from out where the soldiers were watching.

Clouds of steamy white smoke began to mingle with the hotter, darker smoke, but not in any noticeable proportion.

Captain Morris turned to the sergeant. 'Get 'em mounted.' He offered no explanation, nor did the sergeant wait for one.

As the detachment moved out, Al Whitten rode between Crowfoot and Tanyard. He was the only man who twisted in the saddle to watch a thick-bodied wraith run hard in the opposite direction.

Maybe the troopers owed Curtis Glidden nothing, but Al and Tom did; not much, but enough, and in any case there was no place for a prisoner at this time.

Captain Morris kept the scouts with him, rode in a long-spending loop out and around the town so as to approach it from the southeast, and encountered only two people, both older men. They were driving a light wagon behind a fifteen-hundred pound draft horse as docile as a dog. The big animal did not wait to be halted when he saw the dark line up ahead.

The old men looked less surprised at seeing soldiers coming from the direction they had not expected to meet anyone, than they were at the way the column spread until they were between two lines, then closed around them, all without a single order being given.

One of the old men was rawboned, grey as a badger and wearing an old hawgleg sixshooter. The other one was not as rangy but just as grizzled and although he had a Sharp's carbine in both hands made no attempt to cock it as Al Whitten spoke above the background noise of the dying village.

'Too hot for you, gents?'

The larger of the old men replied sharply. 'It ain't no joke. Come sunrise there won't be nothing left including his dry good store and my harness works.'

The other old gaffer asked a question. 'You come up from the south? There's another batch of soldiers east of town. That rumour spread last night.'

No one told him this was the same column, but Captain Morris asked if the cattlemen were still in town. Both old men vigorously nodded. 'Them, and some other idiots as well.' The old man eyed Captain Morris, the three scouts, then also said, 'What took you so long? We finally give up on you ridin' in' and dynamited that log warehouse ourselves ... An' a feller left town hour or so back headin' for that fort back east a ways.'

No one appeared to hear the remark about the rider trying to reach Fort Winfield Scott, every eye was on the old man who had spoken. Finally, Al Whitten said, 'You started that fire?'

'Yep. Six of us. They caught one, shot another feller and me'n Angus here, just barely had time to fling the sticks of powder inside before someone come hollerin' that they'd seen three fellers runnin' like jack rabbits toward easterly away from the warehouse.'

Tom Crowfoot looked at Everett and wagged his head about the risks they had taken – for nothing. Everett stared hard at the old men on the wagon seat and, as usual, said nothing.

Captain Morris asked where the old men were going and got a frank reply. 'Away. Maybe come back in a day or two in case somethin' can be salvaged, but we had enough; damned rangemen ridin' roughshod, makin' the law, actin' like they owned the place ... and now them damned rapid-fire guns. Hell, if the army don't find out about them the Apaches will, an' either way they ain't goin' to just set an' wait. Specially the ragheads.'

Captain Morris nodded and the big draft horse leaned into its collar. The wagon moved, Whitten and Crowfoot exchanged a wry look; that wagon was a toy to the beast pulling it.

Captain Morris sent Al and Tom ahead to scout and waited until they returned. Burnt Timbers was a shambles; the bucket-brigade had managed to save four buildings. The rest of the town was ash and smoke.

The fire brigade was still struggling but the men were exhausted. Captain Morris rode in from the west, left horse-holders and took the rest of his detachment to replace exhausted firemen.

They did not make much of a difference; the town was too far gone, but people watched soldiers trying to salvage something of their settlement and were grateful.

The fire-bright sky had been fading toward dawn for some time without anyone noticing it until a hard-riding band of horsemen suddenly appeared at the upper end of Burnt Timbers heading away in haste. Someone bawled and pointed to the silhouettes, and Al Whitten called to the captain. 'Cowmen!'

Without awaiting an order the grizzled sergeant led the rush down where they'd left their mounts. Captain Morris followed their example. So did the three scouts.

Burnt Timbers' haggard residents would have to take up the slack with their buckets.

By this time a couple of other structures, although damaged by fire, had been saved from complete destruction.

What had been a thriving settlement was down to four structurally sound buildings and two that would require considerable repairing. It was not a total loss, but to those who had been burned out it seemed to be.

Daylight was on the way. Dawn yielded quickly once the sun arrived, but as the Fort Scott detachment went in pursuit of fleeing cattlemen there was no sun and would not be for another hour or so.

Until the pursuit was under way no one'd taken time to look around. Every man was whisker-stubbled, drawn and gaunt looking, their clothing was soiled, wrinkled and smelled strongly of smoke.

Of the entire cavalcade only the pair of 'breeds looked no different than they normally looked, and only one of them seemed as alert and resolute as he had from the beginning: Everett Tanyard did not push his horse, which allowed others to pass him. He rode as though he anticipated an endurance race. Eventually Al Whitten and Tom Crowfoot dropped back to set their gait according to his.

Once away from the village the cold was noticeable, particularly so because of their exertion at the bucket brigade.

The veteran sergeant looked around, then asked if anyone had seen their prisoner. No one replied. The only rider among them who had seen the teamster, kept silent.

No one pressed the subject, least of all the sergeant, who may not have cared that their prisoner had probably escaped. His interest was in the men they were pursuing, and, as he and undoubtedly others had noticed, the cattlemen remained in a group only until they were a mile or so north of Burnt Timbers then, thanks to the brightening new day it was possible to see where bands of them had split off.

Captain Morris called a halt to palaver with his scouts. He did not want to divide his command for the basic reason that there was no way to know whether the cowmen had perhaps split up to meet somewhere in greater numbers.

The upshot of their council was that if they ran down one band of cowmen, they could probably elicit all the information they would need to locate the others.

When they struck out again, this time without haste, Al and Tom Crowfoot sashayed ahead to pick up the best trail, not a difficult undertaking with strengthening daylight to show the way.

The party they finally settled upon running to ground had no less than ten riders, perhaps twelve, in it. The trail led northwest and after a couple of miles it seemed clear that the stockmen had a definite goal in mind. As the veteran sergeant opined, a ranch where he guessed they would be holed up and waiting.

Al Whitten rode ahead, puzzling over the prospect of rangemen taking on the US Army, even a detachment of it; there was no surer way to achieve ruin, not just for the rancher but for any of his riders whose defiance of federal forces would put their pictures and names on wanted dodgers from one end of the country to the other end.

He thought the stockmen had to be desperate to even consider defying the army. He also speculated that since there was no sure way to predict how armed men would act, or react, he had to think in terms of renegades and outlaws.

But the idea of such defiance made him shake his head. There was no way he could imagine that the stockmen could survive their actions, beginning with contracting to buy stolen rapid-firing guns, and ending up with challenging the detail from Fort Scott.

Tom Crowfoot came over to point far ahead where rooftops were barely, but unmistakably, visible. Al sent Tom back to the captain and loped ahead over open grassland until he could make out the buildings better.

The sun was climbing, belated warmth was arriving, and so far there was no haze to the new day so visibility was excellent.

He sat a long time studying the buildings. No smoke arose, there was no sign of movement, his impression was that either the buildings were abandoned or were occupied by armed men who were watching and waiting.

Captain Morris loped up, rested both hands on the swells of his McClellen saddle, squinted and said, 'It'd help like hell if we knew this country. That place looks empty.'

Whitten pointed to the fresh tracks. Empty or not, riders had made a bee-line for that yard earlier. He offered to scout ahead but the captain shook his head. 'We'll enter the yard in full force.'

Whitten looked at him. Morris had come up through the ranks; it had taken a long time to do that, which meant he probably knew as much about ambushes as anyone else.

Everett Tanyard rode up with the sergeant. He made an examination of the distant yard then offered it as his opinion that without cover between where the column now was and the yard, it would be impossible to sneak up over there unless the captain wanted to wait until nightfall.

No one thought the captain would do that, and they were right. He re-set his hat, evened up his reins and barely nodded to the sergeant. 'Company front at a walk.'

The detachment was strung out, and depending on how many stockmen were watching, it might look like too many soldiers, or not enough.

A dog barked, otherwise there was neither sound nor movement up ahead. Tom Crowfoot made a wide sashay and returned to report there were horses in the corrals out behind the log barn, and offered it as his opinion that there would be more horses in the barn.

That did not offer much of a clue as to how many rangemen could be holed up among the buildings. The nearest they could come to making a reasonable guess was from the tracks they had followed to this place. That figure was between ten and twelve, less than half the number of troopers advancing toward the yard.

Captain Morris halted the column out of carbine range but within rifle range, took Whitten and the sergeant and rode at a dead walk toward the yard.

Behind him, troopers dismounted to watch and wait.

About hundred yards from the yard that barking dog ran out of the log barn alternately barking and snarling. None of the oncoming horsemen heeded him, their attention was upon the silent, empty-looking buildings which had been erected in a rough horseshoe shape with the main house at the south end.

It was an old ranch, judging by the trunks of the raffish old cottonwood trees scattered about, and the bone-grey weathered look of the buildings.

The dog stopped barking as the riders came to the edge of the yard, turned and with a tucked tail went back into the barn.

Captain Morris's eyes did not leave the front of the main-house. Whitten and the sergeant shot glances elsewhere. No one came out to greet them, the silence was seemingly endless until they had passed several outbuildings, one of which was the bunkhouse, another was the cook shack. A solitary rangeman appeared on the porch of the cook shack, leaned on a supporting overhang upright and went to work rolling a smoke. He acted as though the three riders were not in the yard.

Captain Morris stopped near the raised porch of the main-house where a long pole tie-rack separated the house from the yard. As he was preparing to dismount someone opened the heavy oaken door and stepped forth.

Both Captain Morris and Tom Whitten stared. It was a woman!

Somewhere behind them the solid hush was broken by the sound of an astonished scout slowly expelling his breath.

Captain Morris removed his hat as he said, 'Good morning, ma'm,' and seemed at a loss of what to say next. He had entered the yard ready to fight, prepared in fact to make a battlefield of the yard.

The veteran sergeant smiled, the only one of the three of them facing the shock of the day, able to recover his aplomb without difficulty. He removed his battered old campaign hat and said, 'If your husband's around, we'd like a word with him, ma'am.'

The woman appeared to be in her early forties. She had a complexion of peaches and cream, very dark, almost violet, eyes, and well-formed even features. Her hair was a mass of reddish-auburn colour and as she shifted her attention from the captain to the sergeant her features remained expressionless as she said, 'I am a widow. My husband died six years ago.' She returned her attention to Captain Morris. 'Would you be kind enough to tell me why those soldiers are out there, and why you are here?'

Al Whitten replied, the captain was still off balance. 'We trailed ten or twelve men to your yard, ma'am. The army would like to talk to them.'

'About what, Mister ...?'

'Whitten. Alan Whitten, scout attached to the army at Fort Winfield Scott. Some stockmen had Gatling guns and ammunition delivered to them at Burnt Timbers. Last night the warehouse with the guns and ammunition caught fire and blew up. We tracked some of the men involved to your yard.'

The handsome woman's eyes widened. 'Gatling guns? Aren't those the ones a man cranks with a handle and they have barrels fixed in a circle so that they fire as the barrels revolve?'

Captain Morris nodded. 'About the men who came into your yard, ma'am ...?'

'Margaret Halsted, Captain. I don't know anything about men coming into my yard this morning.'

'You were here, Mrs Halsted?' the officer asked in a soft voice.

'I was here. I haven't been off the ranch in three weeks. I didn't hear or see ten riders in my yard.'

'How many riders do you keep?' Al Whitten asked.

The woman's attention returned to Whitten. 'Four year-round; this time of year I hire a few more. If you think my riders were involved with those guns, you'll have to hunt them. They left before dawn this morning to start a gather on the northwest range, about six miles from the yard.'

The captain was faintly frowning. 'There were more than ten or twelve cattlemen involved, Mrs Halsted. We picked up the tracks of these particular men first. We'll hunt down the others directly ... Gatling guns are not available to civilians.'

The woman arched perfect eyebrows. 'I didn't know that, but there would be no reason for me to know that. Did you actually find the guns in Burnt Timbers?'

There was an awkward silence before Captain Morris said, 'Burnt Timbers was destroyed by fire when the ammunition blew up.'

This time the handsome woman's shock was noticeable to each one of them. 'Destroyed …?'

'Burned to the ground except for a few buildings, and I think some of them were pretty badly charred.'

The woman went to a chair and sat down.

Captain Morris faced his sergeant. 'Search,' he said curtly. The sergeant turned to obey and in the near distance someone made a loud whistle. Whitten, Captain Morris and the sergeant turned.

Out where the column was standing with their horses several men were waving their hats and pointing with rigidly upflung arms.

# NINE
# Unappreciated Company

It was a solitary horsemen travelling fast in a northeasterly direction. Captain Morris growled for the scouts to pursue him and as they left the yard he turned back toward the woman, speaking in a sarcastic tone of voice. 'When we entered the yard there a man was standing on the cook shack porch; he wasn't there to watch and listen, was he? You wouldn't know anything about that either, would you?'

The woman, whose shock over the destruction of Burnt Timbers was passing, gave the officer look for look. 'What I know, is that the man you saw worked for me. I thought he'd gone out with the others before daybreak until I saw him over there.'

'That's all you know?'

The officer's sarcasm was very noticeable as he lifted his left hand to rein away. The woman stepped to the porch railing and spoke sharply. 'Whether you believe it or not, I don't give a damn. I know nothing about those guns or anyone riding into my yard this morning.'

The captain had the last word. 'Ma'am, you must sleep like the dead.'

With his three scouts fanning it after the hard-riding rangeman Captain Morris had to rely on himself and the sergeant to interpret the sign they saw, which was as easy as falling off a log, actually.

Those rangemen they had tracked to the ranch had

clearly changed animals at the barn and had then resumed their race northwesterly, riding all in a group. It was the sergeant's opinion that Mrs Halsted could have been telling the truth; the main-house was a fair distance from the barn and corrals, it had been dark when the fugitive stockmen had reached her place, and still dark when they had resumed their ride.

Herbert Morris looked sardonically at his sergeant, who was rough and tough, and gallant toward women.

The detachment had been straddling the same horses for more than twenty-four hours, had been able to provide a little graze for them and a little rest, items which would not have revitalized the animals even if they hadn't been in a run after leaving what was left of Burnt Timbers.

Captain Morris watched the distant scouts, reduced to ant-size far ahead in the glass-clear morning, and felt like swearing a blue streak because he could not push the horses in pursuit.

The sergeant was more philosophical. He had a cud in one cheek and was riding loose and relaxed as he too watched the tiny figures near the far-off horizon.

'In a horse race,' he opined, 'that cowboy'll win if he's on a fresh animal.'

It was something Captain Morris did not want to hear.

The rangeman and his pursuers were eventually lost to sight altogether, but the detachment had a broad, fresh trail of running horses to follow.

About an hour later, with the sun still climbing and the land empty-appearing except for distant trees, a faint reverberation of gunshots came down to the troopers.

The veteran sergeant sat straight in his saddle, nostrils flaring like an old firehorse who has caught scent of smoke.

The shooting stopped then was resumed. Captain Morris fixed a position in mind and angled slightly with the troop following.

Everett Tanyard came loping into view. The detail continued on its new course until the dark 'breed came up, halted and with no expression, made his report to the officer. 'His horse up-ended in a prairie dog village. The feller run into some rocks an' trees. Crowfoot an' Whitten got him in there, but he's a long way from givin' up.'

As Captain Morris gestured for Everett to lead the way a trooper asked about the horse. Tanyard looked back. 'Didn't break nothin' which is a wonder, but he'll be couple months gettin' over some strained tendons.'

The veteran sergeant studied the country up ahead through slitted eyes. 'Sure as hell they left him at the lady's yard to watch us.'

The officer's reply was tart. 'Unless she had him stay back while her friends ran for it.'

The sergeant put a reproving look upon the officer but said no more.

The gunfire had stopped, but Everett Tanyard rode with his handgun in his lap as he watched the yonder countryside. When he eventually halted to allow the officer to come up, Tanyard pointed with an upraised arm in the direction of some huge boulders with a scattering of pines and firs among them. It was an ideal defensive position except for one thing: There was one man holed-up in there and two scouts keeping him in there while the entire force under Captain Morris rode up.

He could not have escaped if he'd been able to sprout wings.

Al Whitten led his horse back where the officer was sitting his mount and said, 'His horse dumped him. He's in the rocks. Tom thinks he's about out of ammunition.'

Captain Morris nodded and eased ahead at a slow walk until he was well within hailing distance, then halted and shouted.

'Come out of there. Leave your weapon behind. We're not going to waste much time. If we have to smoke you out, we will.'

There was a long interval of silence, Captain Morris was turning to order his line when Al Whitten called to him, 'Here he comes.'

The rangeman picked his way carefully among the rocks. He used both hands for balance as he progressed and his holster was empty.

Not a word was said. The soldiers watched in silence, as did the scouts and the officer.

The rangeman was weathered, lean and fairly tall. He was badly in need of a shearing but had shaved recently. He stopped at the last tumble of boulders and looked around. Whitten called to him. 'Keep walking, hands in plain sight.'

The stranger left his boulders, stepped clear of the last trees and did not take his eye off the line of soldiers as he advanced toward them.

Tom Crowfoot spoke softly aside to Al Whitten. 'Damned fool.' Al did not press the 'breed for an explanation. It wasn't necessary.

Captain Morris dismounted, stepped to the head of his horse trailing both reins and looked stonily at their captive. 'What's your name?' he demanded.

'Frank Rollie.'

'Where are the others?'

Rollie made an all-encompassing gesture. 'Up in the timbered foothills by now.'

'Where are they heading?'

Frank Rollie let his arm drop, he looked thoroughly disillusioned. 'To the Kirkham place.'

'To make a stand?'

The captive shrugged and said nothing more.

Captain Morris gestured for the sergeant to take their prisoner and swung up across leather as he told the scouts to pick up the trail again.

This time when they had a prisoner he did not have to walk. One of the troopers took him up behind his saddle.

Al Whitten dropped back to talk to the man. His first question had to do with the Halsted woman, and the rangeman dragged out his answers as though this was not a topic he liked to discuss.

'She didn't have nothin' to do with any of it, an' right now I wish I could say the same.'

'Who was the head In'ian?'

'Wizened little feller, older'n dirt. Jamie Kinnock. He's been losin' cattle an' horses, mostly horses, to the rag-heads for a long time. More'n the other ranchers, but when he finally had enough he didn't have no trouble gettin' the others to pitch in with him.'

'Gatling guns?'

Frank Rollie would not look at Al. 'All's I know is that they was comin' to town. Seemed like a big secret about them guns.'

'Haul them over to Apache Canyon?'

'That's right.' The rangeman's eyes swung to Whitten, hard and uncompromising. 'What's it to you, an' these horse-soldiers? Any of you had relatives shot by them bastards, or had your cattle killed and left lying, or your saddle stock run off in the night? Not once, but year after year.'

Al Whitten did not argue. He was not entirely out of sympathy with the stockmen; most folks weren't, but wholesale slaughter down to pups and does was carrying things a lot farther then Whitten, and others, approved of.

He loped ahead where Tom Crowfoot and Everett Tanyard were speaking gutturally. They stopped as soon as Al rode up. Crowfoot said, 'Everett says we're riding into real fine bushwhacking country.'

Whitten slouched along for several hundred yards alternately watching the broad trail they were following and the broken, boulder-strewn and timbered foothills ahead, beyond which rose stair-stepped mountainsides of dark timber. Everett was right; if the cattlemen meant to fight, this would indeed be excellent country to thin out the soldiers as they entered it.

He reined back to the captain and was about to mention
the possibility of an ambush when the officer pointed with
a gauntleted hand and said, 'Scout up through there, the
three of you. If they're waiting I'd like to know it.'

Al, Tom and Everett left the column in a slow lope. The
tracks led straight up into a brushy draw which would hide
men on horseback, and at the mouth of the arroyo Al
halted.

Everett grunted and pointed along the east slope where
the big old over-ripe trees were fairly thick but where
there was no underbrush.

'I'll take up through there,' he stated, and was reining
away before either of his companions could speak.
Crowfoot watched the dark 'breed for a while then turned
his attention to the brushy, dark arroyo and its westerm
rim. 'Good grouse country,' he muttered and Al Whitten
laughed.

Crowfoot slowly straightened in his saddle looking
dead ahead into the treacherous-looking arroyo. He was
still and silent for a moment then spoke softly. 'Ragheads!'

'Where?'

'Watch them chaparral bushes near the mouth.'

Al glanced first over his shoulder, the column was a half
mile away and coming at a walk. He swung his attention
back to the mouth of the canyon but saw nothing.

Everett Tanyard was climbing past the lower hills. He
was passing in and out among forest giants. Al wanted to
yell a warning but Tanyard was too distant. Even if he
heard the warning shout he would be unable to get back
down out of there in time.

'How many, Tom?'

'I saw two, but if there's two there's more. I think
whatever they was up to, the sight of the soldiers diverted
their attention ... Depending on how many they are
whether they'll disappear or try to empty a few saddles.'

Al looked down. The tracks of the cattlemen skirted

the arroyo up the west side, but if those broncos had been down in there when the ranchers went past … 'Not too many, Tom, or they'd have jumped the cowmen.'

Crowfoot remained erect and still. Only when the horses pitched their ears forward and raised their heads in a stance of faint alarm, did anything change.

The Indian who rode up out of the arroyo was not daubed for war, but that did not always mean anything. He was riding a piebald horse in pretty fair flesh, which was not common among Indians, except that this was the time of year when graze and browse were plentiful, even Indian horses could put on a little weight.

The bronco had a carbine slung over his back. He did not appear to have a handgun, but he had a big knife with a beaded sheath and a stag handle.

He approached the scouts without taking his eyes off them. He was an older buck, scarred and lined. When he drew to a halt using his single-rein, he sat like a statue looking from the scouts to the oncoming soldiers. Eventually he said, 'Damn,' in accentless English. He was clearly more disgusted than fearful. He returned his attention to Crowfoot and Whitten, and spoke again. 'Damned soldiers everywhere. If it ain't soldiers its cowmen.'

Crowfoot said, 'What cowmen?'

The bronco pointed rearward. 'Come right up atop us before we knew it.'

'Did they see you?'

'No! But you did.'

'There's nothin' to raid up here, is there?' Crowfoot asked and got a disdainful look from the Apache.

'Hunting party. After meat. You get hungry an' we get hungry. Why so many soldiers?'

'We're after those cowmen,' Al said, and the Indian's dark eyes with the muddy whites swung to him.

'Why? Did they start that big fire?'

Tom Crowfoot saw Everett sitting in the distance

watching them. He raised his arm to signal for Tanyard to return. The dark 'breed obediently turned back, still riding at a walk.

Whitten asked if the Indian had seen the fire. He nodded. 'Everyone saw it. And heard the thunder ... One of our scouts said he saw big guns get blown into the air.'

Al and Tom exchanged a look before Whitten addressed the Apache again. 'Gatling guns. Do you know what a Gatling gun is?'

The Indian surprised them by nodding his head. 'When I pot-hunted for the army a long time ago. I saw Gatling guns.'

'Did you ever see one fired?'

'No.'

'But you know what they can do?'

'Shoot people today and kill them tomorrow.'

'The guns your scout saw were brought here to be wheeled to the rim overlooking your village in the canyon.'

The Indian stared at Whitten. 'By the soldiers?'

'No, by those ranchers you've been raiding for a long time. They figured to end it once and for all with those Gatling guns.

'Those men who ran past the arroyo?'

'That was some of them.'

'And you're going after them with the soldiers?'

'Yes.'

'We will go with you.'

Everett Tanyard was within hearing of that last sentence and answered the Apache in his own language. It was guttural and coarse-sounding. The Indian twisted to watch Everett come up and stop. Everett spoke gruffly to him again, and this time the Indian finally showed expression. 'All right; but we can scout ahead of your soldiers. We know this country better ...'

Everett pointed to the nearing column. 'You stay out of it,' he told the bronco in English. 'You see those soliders? If there's a fight some of them will remember things ... You understand?'

Evidently the hunter understood perfectly, but he turned back to watch the soldiers before speaking again. 'We'll wait. We'll stay far behind and wait. If those Gatling-gun-men get away from you we'll be waiting.'

Before the scouts could protest the Indian turned back the way he had come and within fifteen minutes had disappeared back into the overgrown, gloomy arroyo.

Tom Crowfoot looked back. Captain Morris was loping toward them. Tom sighed. 'He'll love it having Apaches behind his column.'

When the officer came up they told him what they had just encountered. He immediately squinted in the direction of the arroyo but there was nothing to be seen but flourishing stands of thorny chaparral intermingled with red-barked manzanita.

He turned irritably on Al Whitten. 'Why didn't you hold him?'

Al ignored the tone of voice when he answered. 'How; with his friends in the brush watching?'

Captain Morris peered into the canyon again. 'Damned ragheads behind us, gun-handy cowmen in front of us. You know what the major would do? Go back to Burnt Timbers and wait for reinforcements.'

Whitten glanced farther back where the troopers were listening. 'Those damned cowmen'll be out of the country if we go back and wait,' he grumbled.

Captain Morris sat a moment in thought then glowered in the direction of the arroyo. 'Scout ahead. Keep to the tracks on the west side of the arroyo. And keep a close watch on that damned canyon.'

Tom Crowfoot offered minor encouragement. 'Well, those Gatling-gun-men won't set up no ambush. Whether they know there are ragheads down here or not, they'd never get it done before the In'ians saw it and came back to let us know.'

# TEN
# A Surprise in the Night

As the ride was resumed Everett Tanyard looked as dour as he usually looked, and this time with ample reason. During Everett's existence in this vale of tears he had come to believe that if circumstances seemed to be in opposition to the desires of men, they usually were, and they usually managed to make their opposition known, very often in unpleasant ways.

He understood Apaches although he was not an Apache, and while he kept his mouth shut about atrocities he knew why they were committed.

Everett was one of those unique individuals who'd had one way of life destroyed without having any suitable substitute for it presented. Although he was only a quarter whiteskin and had early on recognised the death throes of his forefathers' natural existence and had joined the whiteskins because they were obviously going to be successful conquerors, he was still more redskin than whiteskin.

How he managed to balance upon the knife-edge so well for so long only Everett Tanyard could have explained, and that was something he made no attempt to do, taking refuge in stoic silence.

On this particular scout, however, his burden was lightened because soldiers as well as ragheads were allied against would-be butchers, and perhaps more for this reason than any other he rode in advance of Whitten and Crowfoot, reading sign and making sound judgments, one of which he explained to the other scouts and the captain where the troop halted at a cold-water creek.

There was no sign of the Apaches, he told Captain Morris, which probably meant they were working hard to avoid being seen. Otherwise, there was a hump-backed hill northeasterly which was the direction the fleeing cowmen had taken. It was his guess that beyond the hill there would be open country again, and perhaps that was the destination of their prey since horses could not keep up the pace those men had set indefinitely.

Everett turned back after reporting and left the others gazing at his back as he picked his way among big timber on the fairly fresh trail they had been following most of the morning.

A more-or-less raffishly civilised Tom Crowfoot said, 'He seems almost pleasant.'

Captain Morris, who had known Tanyard a long time, wagged his head and said nothing. But when the ride was continued he rode up beside Al Whitten to make a remark that was fairly close to the truth.

'We're not riding down In'ians, for a change, and we're not going after those ragheads in the arroyo. I suspect he likes the idea of both In'ians and soldiers going after the same enemy.'

Al Whitten, who had also known Everett Tanyard a long time, was watching the scout's back up ahead when he replied. 'I've thought it must be hell on a man from one camp living and working in the other camp.'

Tom Crowfoot waited until the officer and Whitten came up then smilingly jutted his jaw. 'They're behind us.'

Neither listener asked who was behind them because they did not have to. The officer looked up ahead. 'How far behind us?'

'Some slippin' through the trees are closer than the others, but not too far.'

'How many?' Whitten asked, and got another of Crowfoot's wide smiles. 'You can't count 'em when they're slitherin' back and forth. You know that.'

'Make a guess, Tom.'

'Six, maybe eight. Not enough to worry about – except for one thing. By now they've councilled and they all know what the stockmen meant to do with those Gatling guns. One thing you learn early about 'Paches, they're vengeful little bastards.' Crowfoot's smile faded slightly as he started to turn away. 'When they're no longer behind us you can figure they've gone ahead on their own to settle with the cowmen.'

Al and the captain resumed the ride, both watching as Crowfoot rode up ahead within shouting distance of the other, dark scout.

Captain Morris muttered in a low voice, 'If they do, if they find those stockmen before we do, and make a strike, there's not enough of them to do much harm – but if some of them get killed, the In'ians back at the Apache Canyon village will never believe the army didn't have a hand in it.'

Al Whitten leaned to make a swipe at a big deer-fly about to land on his horse's neck before replying to the officer. 'Did you ever ride with ragheads as allies before?'

'No, and if anyone had told me that someday I would, I'd tell him he was crazy.' The officer looked over at his companion with a cold, hard twinkle in his eyes. 'In this life I've learned darned little, but one thing I know for a fact. Don't ever say you wouldn't do something, because sure as hell whatever fate ordains things, will make you do it, will rub your nose in it.'

Al laughed.

The officer and scouts paid little heed to what was behind them, but the troopers did, particularly the veteran sergeant who'd been in skirmishes with Indians most of his enlisted life. Neither he nor the troopers around him put one shred of faith in what Apaches said, and even less in what they might do.

Everett Tanyard was correct. He disappeared around the broad trail that angled along the base of the hump-backed hill without making any attempt to climb or use any of the numerous game trails. Here, the tracks they followed were made in the dust of a very old wagon road. Where it dipped southeasterly, though, the fresh shod-horse marks continued northeasterly around the hill.

When the column rounded the slope they had a big bowl dead ahead. It had timber, but most of all it had miles of grass. The brush which the troopers had encountered now and then south of the hump-backed hill, was confined to the edges of the big valley, evidently burned back that far by people who wanted only grass for feed and a few trees for shade.

Captain Morris called a halt, had the prisoner brought up, and asked if the distant weathered buildings near the northwesterly side of the big valley was the place the stockmen had been heading for.

The prisoner looked, was silent a long time, then grudgingly nodded his head. 'That'll be it. A feller named Kirkham founded it. He died years back and Jamie Kinnock bought it off the widow.' The prisoner could not help but make an observation, regardless of his circumstances, that any stockman would have made.

'You ever see such a natural settin' for livestock? I never have.'

Captain Morris was not a stockman. He had of necessity picked up some knowledge over the years because he'd been stationed in stock country, but as he gazed out over the sunbright meadow his interest was solely in those distant buildings. 'All open country,' he said aloud, to no one in particular. 'As soon as we leave the timber they'll see us.'

No one spoke; whatever decision was to be made was exclusively the captain's to make.

'Find water, Al, but don't go out into the open. 'Water and grass. We'll wait.'

Whitten nodded to Tom Crowfoot. They rode westward through the timber. Of grass for the horses they expected to find either very little or none at all. Where pines and firs grew, shed their resin and resin-impregnated needles, grass did not grow. Even in places where the trees were often as much as a hundred or so feet apart, grass was scarce.

Crowfoot was watching the northerly slope of country toward that huge bowl of grass when he said, 'He's thinkin' about tryin' to get up close after dark.'

Al nodded, he'd already deduced that, and thought beyond it. 'Not with the entire detachment. They'd hear it whether they could see it or not.'

True to their expectations they found a good creek but very little grass. They followed the creek to a stand of creek-willows which horses would eat if they had to, then turned back to report.

The day was dying by the time Captain Morris followed his scouts back to the place for a bivouac, and, as was expected, hungry horses went after those juicy little creek willows like they were rolled barley or crushed oats.

They had food, of sorts, but because there could be no fires they ate it cold, the soldiers had beards of varying textures and lengths. Their uniforms were stained and dirty, even the freshest recruit could have passed as a veteran.

Shortly after a meagre, dry supper several of the troopers who were back a short distance, closer to the trail they had made getting to this place, thought they had heard something, and the sergeant called for Al Whitten to go back down their back-trail. He took Everett with him. Tom Crowfoot was already dozing with his back to a huge old sugar pine.

It was getting dark on the forested slope an hour before dusk arrived out over the grass valley.

Neither Whitten nor Tanyard made a sound as they glided on either side of the trail, and they halted often. In darkness it was easier, and usually safer, to hear things than to try and see them.

They did not have to go very far before they both heard riders. Where the scouts came together on the north side of the trail Al Whitten whispered, 'They're sure pickin' their way.'

Everett nodded, head up and wary. 'Two horses,' he told Whtten, and added something more: 'Two better than twenty.'

'Picked up our sign and been followin' it?' Al asked, and got no answer because by now it was possible to hear the approaching horses very distinctly. Everett Tanyard was as still as a statue as he worked out in his mind the precise location of the invisible riders.

He turned once to whisper. 'I don't think they come up from that big valley.'

All that statement did for Al Whitten was heighten his bewilderment because its alternative notion was that whoever was tracking them had come up from the Burnt Timbers country.

Otherwise it had to be some mountaineer, possibly a pot hunter or wolfer, who had stumbled onto their trail and had followed it out of curiosity.

There were two horses. Mountaineers usually rode one and led a pack animal.

They squatted beside a forest mammoth, where Al Whitten had a suspicion that it would not be mountaineers; men whose lives were spent being as wary as the creatures they hunted. No one in his right mind would ride into an area where he might very well got shot out of his saddle in the dark.

If he was all that curious he would wait for daybreak.

They could hear rein-chains and, finally, an occasional

sound of a steel horseshoe striking rock. The horses were almost within sighting distance, which had to be quite close considering the darkness, deeper among big trees than in open country.

Al brushed Everett's shoulder as he arose and pulled loose the tie-down over his holstered Colt. They were not hidden by their huge tree but they were well camouflaged by it.

The horses came plodding into view, being ridden on slack reins. For a moment or two the riders were not very distinct, but when they finally were both the scouts stopped breathing for a couple of seconds.

Al stepped ahead, stopped in the middle of the trail and said, 'You're a long way from home, ma'am.'

Margaret Halsted was so startled by his abrupt appearance she yanked her horse back, hard. The rider behind her also made an abrupt halt. All Al Whitten saw was the handsome woman on the lead animal. As Everett Tanyard came soundlessly into sight the second rider snarled at him in a coarse language that stopped Everett in his tracks with a deep scowl. 'Speak English,' he growled, and the second rider did; she swore fiercely at him in English until he walked back, grabbed her arm and yanked her out of the saddle.

The Halsted woman twisted in her saddle. 'Take your hand off her!' she said coldly.'

Everett obeyed but continued to glower at the second woman, a sturdy, short and dark Mexican, who now tried Spanish, another language Everett did not understand. He blew out an exasperated breath and repeated his earlier statement: 'Speak English!'

Al Whitten moved up beside the lead horse. 'What are you doing over here?' he asked, thoroughly baffled by the appearance, and the identity of the woman looking down at him from her saddle.

'Trailing you,' she responded in the same cold voice.

'Why? You rode all that distance – why?'

'Because after you left I rode out to find my riders. They were not up where they were supposed to be. Their tracks showed that they had not been out there at all. They were riding with those men you are looking for.'

A quiet, steady voice spoke from among the trees where Captain Morris walked into sight. 'We suspected that, Mrs Halsted. I'm still having trouble believing you didn't know those men rode into your yard, switched to fresh horses and rode out – without you hearing anything. But maybe you've provided the answer: If your men were with the others, they would know how to make that change without awakening you … It still doesn't seem reasonable, but for the time being I'll accept it.'

The handsome woman looked coldly at the officer who came up and halted at the head of her horse. 'How very kind of you,' she said.

'Kindness had nothing to do with it,' the captain stated. 'If you'd been tied in with those renegade stockmen, you wouldn't have tracked us, you would have gone down across that valley to warn the stockmen how close we are.'

The officer nodded past in the direction of the irate sturdy dark woman still facing Everett Tanyard. 'Who is that?' he asked.

'Her name is Emily Carrera. She is my housekeeper.'

Captain Morris, still sounding sarcastic, said, 'I admire loyalty, Mrs Halsted.'

'She is also my friend and companion, Captain.'

'I see. Well, now that you are here we all might as well return to camp. We don't have much food but we can fix both of you a comfortable place to rest. You must be very tired.'

For a moment it seemed that Margaret Halsted might refuse, but when Al Whitten said, 'Your animals need rest more than you do,' she acquiesced with a frosty smile. 'Thank you, Captain. We'll start back in the morning.'

The presence of two woman compounded the captain's problems, but he did not allow it to show as he led the way back to the camp where wide-eyed men watched them pass in silence.

Not until later, when Al and Everett went among the soldiers, was their curiosity put to rest, but only partially. As the sergeant grumbled, a man, let alone a female-woman, wouldn't do what those two had done just to pass a warning that some of the renegade rangemen up ahead had been working on a local ranch, something everyone had already assumed long ago.

That made Al Whitten wonder, but as he, Everett and Tom Crowfoot prepared to roll into their blankets Al thought about it, conjured up several ideas and when none of them seemed applicable, he put the entire affair out of his mind and went to sleep.

The captain, whose entire responsibility this pursuit was, was less sanguine. He kept the two women sitting in night-chill while he tried to ferret out what he thought had to be a motive other than the one they had related, as their reason for making such an arduous ride.

Like his men, he was not quite prepared to believe they had made that exhausting ride just to tell him what he had long suspected. But the captain, like his whiteskin scout, did not know very much about women. Particularly strong-willed ones.

He did learn a couple of things he had not known before. One was that Margaret Halsted had told the truth about not leaving her ranch in three weeks, the reason being that she'd heard rumours concerning the intentions of the other ranchers to go after the Apaches in force and in a surprise raid, something she did not approve of because for the last six or eight months the Indians had not been troublesome and she had some idea that this might presage a gradual ending of the Apache wars in her territory.

The other thing Captain Morris learned was that Jamie Kinnock's scheme hadn't plenty of support among the cattlemen, he was not, personally, very popular among them. It was her opinion that if Kinnock could be eliminated one way or another, the other stockmen would not press for that attack on Apache Canyon.

Captain Morris asked for details about Kinnock, which Margaret Halsted supplied from an acquaintanceship stretching back long before her husband's death. The verbal picture she offered did not incline the captain to consider this man he had never met, very favourably.

She knew most of the other stockmen too, but her opinion of most of them was not particularly bad. They had simply decided to end what had been a constant source of loss going back more years than she thought most human beings would have put up with.

Except for two men. One named Hyrum Kaster, the other named Bert Kindig, who were not stockmen at all, they were hired gunfighters masquerading as rangemen in Jamie Kinnock's employ.

The captain asked a sentry to cut boughs and make pallets for the women, and smiled at Emily Carrera. 'That scout who pulled you off the horse is Northern Cheyenne. Aside from English and a smattering of Apache, he's pretty limited in language skills.'

The dark woman's reply was sharp. 'He understood enough Apache when I swore at him.'

The captain laughed. '*Senõra*, have you ever heard that the first words a man learns in a foreign language are the bad ones?'

She smiled back because she had heard that at least a dozen times during her lifetime. 'If he understood Spanish, Captain, he would have done more than yank me off the horse.'

The dark woman flicked a glance at Margaret Halsted then back to the officer. 'That scout – not the Indian, the other one. He lives at your fort?'

'Yes'm. All the scouts live at Fort Scott.'

'He lives with his wife at your fort?'

Captain Morris softly frowned. 'None of our scouts have wives.'

As the officer arose to go over where bedding was being arranged for the women, Margaret Halsted looked bleakly at her companion. 'That wasn't necessary, Emily.'

The dark woman shrugged. 'Unless a person asks questions how do they find things out?' When the Halsted woman would have spoken again Emily Carrera held up a hand. 'Don't worry. I just wanted to know whether we had made such a ride for nothing.'

'Emily, what are you talking about?'

'*Señora*, I am past fifty; I've known men and I know why a woman looks at a certain man in a particular way ... May we not get some rest?'

The captain returned to escort them to their pine-bough pallets, which were well away from the troopers but not so far that a patrolling sentry would not pass by every half hour or so.

When the officer got back to his own bedroll the veteran sergeant was smoking a foul little pipe which he removed as the captain sat down, and said, 'Do we leave them here in the morning, which means we'll have to detach someone to watch them, or do we take them along?'

Captain Morris was tugging at his holstered weapon and belt when he replied. 'Leave them here. We can spare one man,' then he swore under his breath. 'In'ians behind us, forted up renegades in front of us, and now these darned woman.'

The sergeant waited out that remark before asking just how they would cross all that open grassland to reach the buildings.

The officer was tugging off his boots when he replied. 'There's only one way. Strung out in skirmish order and riding at a walk. Give them a good look at what they're going up against, and give them plenty of time to reconsider.'

The sergeant knocked dottle from his pipe and pocketed it. He had anticipated that answer because he had not been able to come up with anything different, but he did not like the idea. There had been times during his service when he'd have preferred Indian strategy to whiteskin strategy and advancing across open country with guns waiting at the other end, as now, was one of those times.

But he said nothing as he arose to head for his blankets. Like Al Whitten, with whom he had ridden many times, his hitch would be up in another six weeks and this time he was not going to re-enlist. Like Al Whitten, he'd had enough soldiering. They had discussed this over some illict popskull several times, but he had not mentioned it to another soul.

Alan had; he'd told Tom Crowfoot he'd had enough. Tom had accepted it; sooner or later they all got enough.

# ELEVEN
# Through The Night

It was darker than the inside of a boot when Everett Tanyard punched Whitten and Crowfoot awake. There were a million stars high in a pitchblende sky, not a breath of wind and the silence was deep and endless.

Everett squatted with his back to the orderly lumps farther off and used *wibluta* to convery his purpose: The three of them would have plenty of time before dawn to cross that prairie and scout up the buildings.

Crowfoot rubbed his eyes and leaned to whisper. 'Cap'n will have fits if we're not back before sunrise.'

Tanyard remained expressionless as he gazed at Tom. He only whispered when Al Whitten said, 'Where are those damned ragheads?'

Tanyard smiled very faintly. 'They'll be up there. It's not their nature to sleep away the best part of a night made for stalking.'

Crowfoot rolled his eyes. 'You're crazy, Everett. If the ragheads don't get us them stockmen might, an' we'll be too far off to get help.'

Tanyard leaned very close as he said, 'If they don't already know we're up here in the trees, they will know it the minute we ride down out of here and form up in their direction. You might as well blow a bugle.'

A sentry passed among the trees lower down the slope and did not even look in the direction of the scouts. He

112

moved like a sleep walker, his stride measured, his body balanced from the waist up, his head fixed in one direction, straight ahead.

Some horses stamped and there was a soft sound of intermittent snoring among the slumbering lumps. Someone coughed, noisily cleared his pipes and lapsed back into silence. Everett whispered, 'I'll go alone,' and leaned to arise.

Crowfoot swore in a whisper, Al Whitten reached for his coiled shellbelt and holstered sidearm, and Everett Tanyard squatted like a dark Buddha waiting.

Leaving the bivouac was no particular problem. There were several sentries but only one of them, a younger man, was completely alert, head swinging, carbine balanced across his body in both hands, and they lay flat as rocks until he had passed, then crawled a few yards, sat up, listened to the young sentry pace back, waited until the sound was lost, got up into a crouch and went down the slope to the edge of a fringe of underbrush where they pushed through to open grassland.

Here, they did not have to whisper, but they whispered anyway. Crowfoot squinted and said, 'It's two, three miles.' Everett agreed. 'About that,' he said, and led off in a loose trot.

Al Whitten did not look back; he watched the onward country and both sides. Like Everett Tanyard he thought the Apaches would be up ahead somewhere. He also thought they would probably pick up reverberations from the ground, or skyline three trotting scouts. Whatever else a man thought of ragheads, they deserved his respect for an ability to detect enemies as well as did coyotes and wolves. Except that this time the trio of trotting men were not enemies; at least they did not think of themselves as enemies. But in darkness an Apache had nothing but enemies, according to his lights, and for a fact nine times out of ten he would be correct.

Everett stopped only once, that was when they came to

marshy ground near a sluggish little warm-water creek.

The three men drank sparingly then stood looking and listening.

They knew where those distant buildings were but as yet were unable to see them. Tom leaned to speak to Everett. 'They'll be up there by now. I don't like the notion of comin' up behind 'em. Ragheads shoot first and look afterwards.'

Tanyard showed no concern as he crossed the creek and started trotting again. Al Whitten had all the faith in the world in Tanyard's tracking ability, but this was different; they weren't tracking nor moving according to sight, they were closing the distance between two kinds of trouble, either of which could be fatal.

Tom grunted, brushed Everett's arm and halted. Dimly discernible ahead was a light. It did not waver nor rise and fall; it was not an outside fire, it was a lamp burning in a place where no wind stirred.

Tom shook his head. 'The ragheads'll zero in on that like gnats.'

Al watched the light for a few moments, then addressed Everett. 'Anyone who did all the schemin' they did isn't that stupid.'

Everett nodded, and led off on a more westerly course without explaining what he had in mind, but Al made a guess: Whether the forted-up rangemen knew how close pursuit was or not, they certainly knew they had left tracks to this place a blind man could follow, which meant they also knew anyone looking for them would follow those tracks, and that, Al thought, also meant that if they intended to slip away in the darkness as he and his companions had done, they would have a choice of going due north or east.

Otherwise why had they left a lamp burning? To draw their pursuers to the ranch buildings up ahead.

He did not know why Tanyard had chosen to angle westerly but speculated that if he intended to go north later, going around the buildings to the west would serve a dual purpose, it would allow them to discern which direction the cowman had gone. If north Tanyard would see their sign. If he saw no sign, they would have gone east.

Tom hissed a sharp warning and dropped to the ground. Whitten and Tanyard did the same. They were lying almost shoulder to shoulder.

There was nothing to see and not a sound. Tom Crowfoot wrinkled his nose. His companions tried to detect the scent that had alarmed Crowfoot and failed. Everett, though, was willing to believe Tom had picked up the gamey scent of ragheads, and Al Whitten was equally ready to believe it, but for a different reason; they were close enough now to be able to make out dark, square outlines where buildings stood, and as far as Whitten was concerned, the Apaches would be up there – somewhere.

The trick was to find them before they found the scouts. As Tom had said back a mile and a half, ragheads shot first and looked second.

Everett raised his head and cupped his hands to make a night-bird cry. Al was watching and saw the blur rise into the air in a lunge. Whitten rolled swiftly, shoved his gunbarrel straight out and braced. When the Indian came down atop the steel barrel he made a rasping gasp and fell against Everett, whose big knife was out in a second. Tom Crowfoot rolled away and got into a crouch, but the Apache was clutching his middle and sucking air as he writhed.

Whitten leathered his sixgun, rolled the Indian onto his back and saw how the man's eyes were rolled back, his mouth was twisted to gulp breath, and disarmed the Apache.

Everett looked down. 'Mating instinct strong in night birds,' he said without any expression. He reached, got a fistful of lank, unwashed black hair and jerked the

Apache into a sitting position. The bronco was recovering, but very slowly. Everett released the man, who fell back in a foetal position both hands clutching his soft parts.

Of one thing the scouts were certain; this was not the older buck they had palavered with back at the brushy arroyo.

It also confirmed for a fact what all of them would have bet a year's wages on hours earlier: That the Apaches had never intended to let the cavalry do what they saw as their thoroughly justified course of action.

The bronco was beginning to breathe again when an owl called from the left somewhere. Al hooted back twice. There was no other sound.

Their injured Indian asked for *tizwin*, which they did not have. They did not even have water along let alone anything stronger, but the fact that he could talk was encouraging.

Tom Crowfoot asked him in his own language where his friends were. He answered by gesturing widely with one arm while still clutching his middle with the other hand.

Tom asked why they hadn't done as their spokesman had said back at the brushy arroyo – stay behind the soldiers. This time Crowfoot got a disdaining look and some guttural, breathy kind of curt reply, which he interpreted for Tom and Al.

'He says them Gatling-gun-men belonged to them, not to us. He said his companions will find them before we do, an' what they'll leave for us a man could pack into one gunny sack.'

Crowfoot looked at Al. 'I thought the captain had trouble when them women rode in ... What do we do with him?'

The Indian surprised his captors by speaking in clipped English. 'I can go with you. Help you.'

Everett spat to indicate his contempt. He said nothing, though, and Tom regarded their prisoner solemnly. He was a strong, muscular buck in his prime, a full-blood with the features that went with it. He smelled gamey enough not to have been near a creek in quite a spell. Crowfoot retrieved the bronco's knife and shoved it into his own belt.

'Al ...?'

Whitten knew what was customarily done, but this time the Apache had been on the side of the army and, he thought, territorial law, splitting his skull was out of the question. On the other hand ...

Everett, who had turned away in disdain when the Apache had made his offer, solved Al Whitten's dilemma by turning back and bringing his Colt down in an overhand strike that stretched the Apache in the grass with a few twitches. They left him tied and face down with a trickle of blood coursing down one cheek from the wound in his scalp. When he regained consciousness he would have the granddaddy of all headaches.

All they had learned from the bronco was that the Apaches were out there, which they already knew.

The lamp up ahead still glowed. Now it was noticeably limned by four frames around a window. It had been deliberately placed there as sure as the fact that dawn would be along directly.

When they resumed their scout they were more careful than ever, not the least worried about the men among the buildings, but very worried about the silent wraiths one of which they had left back a ways dead to the world.

The closer they got the more convinced Whitten became that the lighted lamp had been a deliberate ruse and the buildings were empty.

An owl hooted again. This time it was east and slightly north of the ranch yard, and this time when the answer came it was not two hoots, it was one, and this one came from the northwest.

Tom grunted. 'They got the place covered to the east an' west.'

Tanyard hunkered in tall grass for a long time before
arising as he said, 'Which way, Al?'

Whitten did not hesitate. 'East.'

'Why not north?'

Whitten did not know the country north of the grass
valley, but he had learned recently that east and
southward there were cow outfits with fresh horses,
grub, water, and very likely friends of the renegades
they were pursuing.

Tanyard smiled. It was such a rarity that Tom and Al
stared. Tanyard turned to continue their scout, this time
more eastward. His companions never did figure out
what he'd smiled about.

Al was not as tired as he was hungry. Tom Crowfoot
held up a small hard-cured little pouch. 'Hold out your
hand. I took this off Helping Hand back yonder. I never
liked the stuff but a hungry man don't really have no
likes nor dislikes, does he?'

Whitten did not like it either, but, like his companion,
he chewed it. Dried and pummeled stringy deer and
antelope meat was bearable, but when leached juniper
berries were pounded into the mixture, it was
questionable whether a town dog would have eaten the
stuff unless he'd been on the verge of starvation.

Everett Tanyard was leery and kept his companions
on the outskirts of the yard for a long time without
explaining that he was sure the Apaches were already
either in the house with the lamp, or close enough to go
inside. He had no more desire to be shot at by mistake
than his companion had.

Eventually Al Whitten said, 'Leave 'em ransack the
house. Let's head east.'

Everett nodded and glided to the right of the building
leaving plenty of space between the scouts and the yard.
He picked up the trail without much difficulty. If the
stockmen had been afoot it would have been harder to
do, but they were a-horseback.

They trotted again and by the time it was no longer possible to see the light or the buiding it was in, they had a good trail, night or no night.

Everett coursed ahead and came about as close as he would ever come to losing 'face'.

They were beginning to encounter scraggly stands of thorny chaparral about a mile past the abandoned building back yonder when Everett seemed to hesitate before resuming his course.

Neither Whitten nor Crowfoot had time to question his hesitation. From somewhere up ahead a gunshot sounded, its orange-tinted muzzleblast blinking on and off too rapidly for the surprised scouts to place it.

The bullet may have been close but they neither heard it nor felt it as they dropped like stone and frantically rolled in expectation of another shot, but there was none.

Tom Crowfoot swore under his breath. When he came up close to Whitten he said, 'Son of a bitch! They should have been five miles away by now.'

Everett crawled over and Crowfoot gave him a disgusted glare. Their problem was simple: Whoever had fired at them was probably still in the underbrush up ahead, but whether he was or not they would have to lie flat for a long time before venturing to crawl toward the thicket and that meant lost time.

Also, the ragheads back yonder would have heard that gunshot.

Whitten told his companions he was going to circle around to the south. They said nothing as he crawled away, but as soon as he was out of sight Tom Crowfoot scolded Everett for leading them into an ambush. Tanyard said nothing, although he'd obviously had some kind of intuitive warning back where he had hesitated.

A fair distance westerly an owl hooted and Tom Crowfoot swore and glared at his companion. 'Damned

ragheads'll be coursing past us,' he said, and Everett
held up a hand.

A night bird made its mournful cry from the
chaparral. Everett jerked his head to lead the way. The
bird-sound had been very realistic – except that there
would not be a night bird within a mile of where that
gun had gone off.

When they found Al he was facing southeasterly, and
without palavering led off in a trot. Again, it was not
difficult to follow the trail because, this time, large
animals pushing through underbrush had left a path of
broken limbs.

Where they eventually broke out of underbrush Al
held up his hand. They heard a horse in front of them
moving at what sounded like a trot. Crowfoot smiled.
'He'd have done better just to go along with the others.
All he could hope for was to stall us for a while, an' that
wasn't enough.'

From this point on their gait increased. They were
tough, hardy men. It had been proved many times that a
two-legged creature travelling light and with plenty of
time could out-last a horse.

Everett and Crowfoot travelled side by side. Al
Whitten was out in front, the position Tanyard had
sacrificed by his blunder back yonder.

They were wraiths, seemingly tireless and unerringly
following a good trail.

When Al halted and threw up a hand, all three of
them could hear men up ahead, their voices audible
enough but their words undistinguishable.

Whitten knelt to listen. It did not make sense for
fleeing mounted men to halt miles from the nearest
ranch yard or settlement when they had to realise they
had enemies somewhere behind them.

Right up to the time a man with a bull-bass voice said,
'The hell with that. We're all that's left. We ain't goin' to
win out against what's back yonder waitin' for daylight

to track us. If we stay together they'll run us down sure
… Split up, every man for hisself. Me, I'm for Messico as
fast as I can get down to the border.'

There was another, softer, less noisy voice raised in
dissent, but to the listening scouts this man seemed
nowhere nearly as angry as the man with the loud voice
had been, but they could not make out any of his words,
and as Whitten was starting forward again, they heard
the horsemen resuming their southeasterly course, all in
a group, so whether the bull-bass-voiced dissenter was
with them or not, most of the other men still rode
together.

There was a thin sliver of pale light against the far
curve of the world. It would widen very slowly, but for a
fact daylight was coming.

They were in open country again, seemingly miles of
it without thickets or any trees. Eventually, they would
be seen as they would also see the riders. Their sole
advantage was lying prone in tall grass which would
conceal them, but tall grass did not turn bullets.

Everett hissed and pointed. Dimly obscure up ahead
were horsemen riding at a walk. Only the fact that there
was movement against the gun-barrel-coloured sky
made them noticeable.

Crowfoot wagged his head. What had troubled him
since they'd left the lighted ranch building far back was
the fact that although he had initially thought the
stockmen would have abandonded the ranch sooner,
and should therefore have been miles ahead, obviously
this was not the case, which in turn meant the stockmen
had not left the ranch much before the scouts and
Apaches had arrived back there.

To Crowfoot this was the height of stupidity. The
stockmen had to have known they were being pursued.
He let go of the subject by telling himself that what the
renegade cattlemen had not known, was how close the
pursuit was, and without Crowfoot knowing this is

exactly what had happened, it was the truth. They hadn't known; what had prompted them to eventually abandon the old building was anxiety coupled to the fact that they needed fresh mounts.

By now the soldier-column was moving; Captain Morris knew his scouts were gone and sooner or later, as he cautiously approached the empty buildings, he would probably come across that raghead in the grass with a lump on his head the size of a pullet egg.

What had begun as an endurance race remained as one, except that while the column was leading three unridden horses, the men who owned those animals were belly-down in the grass watching a band of troubled rangemen up ahead halt to have another argument, and this time they did split up, several riders going off on their own trail until what was left amounted to four riders, and as these resumed their southeasterly course, the scouts arose to follow, but at a greater distance because dawn was breaking.

# TWELVE
## Open Country

Crowfoot thought they should sit down and await the arrival of the soldiers, which was a valid idea except for one thing. As Al Whitten said, if those four stockmen up ahead got among their friends, and sure as hell that was what they were aiming for, it would not be just four men, it could be a lot more.

Tom said, 'Well, if it's more let the soldiers handle it.'

Everett Tanyard, silent until now, made a short comment. 'We can get four. We can do it before they get to their friends.'

Crowfoot's eyebrows shot up. 'How? You see that sunshine coming?' He gestured, they were in the middle of an ocean of grass with no cover. Visibility was steadily improving.

Everett jutted his jaw eastward. 'We go away from them, then come down around in front of them.'

His companions stared at him. They'd been jogging most of the night, what Everett was suggesting was more of the same, only covering maybe twice as much distance, maybe even three times as much.

Whitten looked out where those four riders were getting smaller by the minute. He was about to turn back and tell Everett what he thought of his suggestion, when a wisp of movement caught his eye. He settled lower, parted grass stalks very carefully and hissed under his

123

breath. That older bronco they had met at the mouth of
the brushy canyon the previous day was standing like a
statue no more than a hundred and fifty feet away
looking at those disappearing distant horsemen. He had
both arms crossed over his chest and while he seemed to
Tom Crowfoot to be deep in thought, he also seemed to
be enjoying the sight of those distant renegade
stockmen.

Everett Tanyard brushed Al Whitten with his
fingertips. All three of them watched the Apache
behind them, close enough to strike with a stone. While
they were watching him he quietly said, 'You come long
way.' As they sat up in the grass he grinned at them. 'A
man always watch back-trail.' Having expressed this
admonition the Indian walked closer and squatted down
as he made a wide-ranging gesture with one arm. 'You
couldn't catch them. Too far ahead, no cover, bright
sun.' He lowered his arm, still indulgently smiling. 'We
heard them back this way.'

Al asked where his companions were. The older
Indian said they were riding to get around in front of
those fleeing cattlemen. Their intention was to turn the
stockmen back.

When he finished explaining that he looked at each
scout individually before asking who hit one of his men
from behind, and when no one replied, he said, 'He is
back at that house. We'll get him on our way back. Hit
pretty hard an' he lost his knife.'

The bronco was staring at the stag handled big knife
in Tom Crowfoot's waistband. Tom lifted out the knife
and tossed it to land at the Apache's feet. 'He come onto
us ready to fight.'

'He didn't know who you were.'

'Well; we didn't know who he was,' Crowfoot replied,
then changed the subject. 'You think you can turn them
ranchers back? How many riders you got down there?'

'Enough,' the bronco replied.

Crowfoot was disposed to argue. 'Most you got down there is maybe five, six men.'

'There are only four of those renegades.'

Crowfoot smiled without a shred of humour. 'Yeah; an' two of them most likely are hired gunfighters.'

The bronco nodded. '*Muy matador*,' he murmured, looking steadily at Crowfoot. 'We'll see. This is our country. We know many ways to keep it.'

Al Whitten had warm sun on his back and yawned. Everett had not taken his eyes off the Apache since the man had appeared. The blood was the same, the environment hadn't been. Everett spoke to the older man in his native language and drew a blank, hard stare, which he had rather thought might happen. Indians were as varied as were other people. The bronco said something in his own language and Everett wagged his head. The two of them seemed to accept the only language they could converse in as one of fate's ironies; both their tribesmen had fought hard against the users of a language who were dedicated to their destruction.

Indians were not given to nuances nor subtleties, but these two sat looking at one another understanding perfectly, and the older Indian showed worn-even white teeth in a smile as he addressed Everett Tanyard.

'Someday everyone will be the same. But not yet, so we fight. Indian against the whites. This time the whites with Indians.'

Everett said nothing. He was never talkative, but in a conversation like this one, which was philosophical instead of being practical, Everett Tanyard's silence indicated his disinterest.

The bronco had some shag tobacco which he offered around. No one accepted his offer. He made quite a display of being able to roll a smoke as whitemen did. He lighted it and trickled smoke, looked southward where sunlight was beginning to brighten the world toward a mild haziness, and said, 'They are coming back.' He arose. 'Now I go back, find soldiers and bring them here.'

He departed in a jogging gait. The scouts sat and watched him go. Tom said, 'Old bastard's got a horse back there somewhere.'

Al did not doubt this. As he watched the Indian he wagged his head. 'They're pretty good strategists. Some of 'em are, anyway ... What's his name?'

Neither Crowfoot nor Tanyard replied. If they had ever heard the bronco's name they did not remember it. Everett twisted to look back, and grunted.

There were riders, small in the distance but exactly as the bronco had said, they were retracing their route. Tom Crowfoot was not as intrigued by this as he was concerned with their position. He told Al and Everett that if they jumped up and ran, sure as hell those distant horsemen would see them. They might not be able to identify them at that distance, but three men running away ahead of the riders would certainly be interpreted as enemies; all those renegade stockmen had behind them were enemies.

Everett got lower in the grass, said something about trading his horse for a carbine, and became almost invisible as he got belly down.

Crowfoot also sank from sight, but Al Whitten remained squatting. He tried to locate the Apaches who had turned those cattlemen back and could not see a single horseman.

Tom grumbled at him. 'Get down. They're goin' to pass east of us. With luck we'll be safe ... Can you make out if they got Winchesters?'

Al nodded. 'They got 'em. Where are those damned ragheads behind them?'

Tom was not interested in the Apaches. 'Get down!'

Al sank lower in the tall grass, but very slowly. He had finally seen two horsemen farther back, one to the east, the other one to the west of the returning stockmen, but that was all he saw.

Everett muttered, 'You don't see 'em unless they want you to.' Everett parted grass to watch the oncoming ranchers. With Winchesters they could have ended everything before the ranchers saw them. But they had no Winchesters, only hand guns.

Al thought he recognised one of those cowmen, a slight, wiry individual. He could not remember his name but was sure this was the same man who had been with the wagons when he and Tom had been prisoners.

The slight man was loping along beside a thick-shouldered man whose unshorn grey hair showed the brim of his hat. Behind those two a pair of younger men loped along riding twisted in their saddles watching their back trail.

Those two shagging Apaches were a long way back, prudently beyond Winchester range, and now there were six of them, two on the left and two on the right, evidently to dispute any reversal the stockmen might attempt. The other two were directly ahead behind the ranchers.

The Apaches had saddleguns, which they would not have been without if they had been members of a hunting party as the older bronco had said. It would have been unnatural for them to be riding anywhere without saddleguns. The only difference between a raghead hunter and marauder was the direction in which he was facing.

Everett nudged Tom Crowfoot. The stockmen's route was becoming more easterly, their obvious intention to try and out-distance their pursuers while at the same time angling around, perhaps with some idea of getting back to areas where they had friends and allies.

They were going to pass the scouts roughly a hundred and fifty yards to the east.

Al thought of Curtis Glidden, the teamster. If he had been out here he would have cursed men, ragheads or renegades, who were using horses as hard as these riders were doing.

Tom must have been thinking along these lines because, as he watched the stockmen, he said, 'Those damned fools are goin' to end up on foot if they keep that up.'

What puzzled Al was why, if the stockmen had seen only two, perhaps four, Apaches, they had fled from them instead of fighting past. The answer, which he did not know at this time, was simple: The stockmen had not seen just two or four ragheads, there had been all but two of the entire hunting party. Too many to fight past.

Those other Indians were nowhere in sight as the ranchers loped past on tired horses, then drew down to a steady walk and spoke back and forth as they gauged the distance between themselves and the six broncos they had in sight.

Everett was as still as a lizard peering through the parted grass and cursing to himself because he did not have his Winchester.

Tom Crowfoot was also still and belly-down, but he was concerned only with the possibility that those stockmen might turn westerly, in which case they would ride right over the prone men in the grass.

The sun was high, the day was warm and would probably have been warmer but for a spindrift of high thin clouds.

Thirst became a minor problem for the still and motionless men in the tall grass as they drew their handguns and waited.

The cattlemen decided to continue bearing around eastward, which was a relief to the scouts, but which was also a source of frustration; the ranchers were already on the very limit of handgun range and as the scouts watched, they widened that distance to the point that, except for the noise they would make, their sixguns were useless.

Al Whitten had the feeling that they were being left behind in whatever would happen out there in the grassland. The distant Apaches had begun to close the distance. All six of them were getting closer and although the stockmen had stopped pushing their animals, the Indians kept right on loping, anxious, it seemed to Al, to close the distance before much more time had passed.

This would of course force the stockmen to pick up their gait too. Whether they were overtaken or not, they had to stay far enough ahead to be out of Winchester range.

Al rose into a sitting position, head and shoulders above the grass. Tom Crowfoot frowned about this but eventually also sat up. Everett was the last to expose himself. He thought they were still in carbine range, but the stockmen were not looking directly behind them, they were watching the oncoming Indians south of them.

Al spat cotton, ignored his thirst and watched the Indians alter course so as to eventually confront the stockmen. To Whitten it was like having a front-row seat at some kind of game.

None of the scouts looked over their shoulders until a distant, faint shout came from that direction. The Apaches also heard it and stopped stone-still while the ranchers boosted their animals into another lope and either did not hear the shout, nor have any interest in why their pursuing ragheads had stopped beyond the fact that they had halted, which offered the stockmen an opportunity to widen the distance while bearing around more to the southeast again.

The shout had been made by an Indian astride a spotted horse. He was coming ahead at a fast gait. Behind him a fair distance, was Captain Morris's column, loping but not pushing their animals beyond that gait.

It was a big country with excellent visibility, Captain Morris was satisfied with the outcome of the chase. There was no timber, no field of boulders, just open grassland for more miles than a man could see. He rode with his sergeant, thoughtfully calculating and puzzled by only one thing; back among those buildings they had found an injured Indian and abundant sign of a fairly large party of forted-up ranchers. What he saw ahead was four men to the east and several motionless ragheads watching his column advancing.

The Indian leading the way soon out-distanced the troopers. Everett arose out of the grass and stood watching the older Apache ride up. Al and Tom also arose, expecting the Indian to halt. He didn't, he slackened pace long enough to gesture rearward then rode on past in the direction of the other Apaches.

Everett made a good guess: 'He wants them away from here before the fight starts.'

Tom sniffed. 'What fight? Them damned ranchers on their wore-down horses might as well quit right now, otherwise the army's goin' to overtake them, and if they was the best guns in the country, they wouldn't stand a chance once them troopers get in gun range.'

It was a reasonable observation. Captain Morris neither slackened nor increased his gait and he was gradually closing the distance.

Al Whitten almost felt sorry for the ranchers. Their animals were faltering badly now. The riders halted in a tight little group. Al would have given a new hat to hear what they were saying as the blue column came steadily ahead.

Tom crowed. 'It's over an' they know it,' but Everett Tanyard was not convinced. 'They might hang if they let themselves get caught. In their boots I'd fight as long as I could.'

The troopers dropped down to a jolting trot. Al, Tom and Everett were watching both renegade ranchers and troopers and missed seeing the Apaches loping straight southward until they were small in the distance. Al's guess had been correct, the older buck did not want his companions anywhere around if there was a fight.

Morris and his sergeant saw their scouts a fair distance southward and ignored them in favour of watching the four bunched-up riders to the southeast, who were no longer moving as they stonily watched the column of blue-bellies approach.

Captain Morris raised his right arm, the troop halted within Winchester range of the stationary stockmen, and the officer allowed a long moment to pass before calling to the stockmen to get down off their horses, drop their weapons and not to move.

He was obeyed.

Morris said something to his sergeant and the non-commissioned officer growled at the troopers nearest him, then led off at a walk in the direction of the four stockmen standing together in the middle of nowhere.

Captain Morris split his remaining troopers, one part circling up and around the captives, the other part heading toward the scouts with three troopers leading three riderless horses.

The soldier who tossed reins to Al Whitten looked disapproving but said nothing. Another trooper, older and more faded, growled at Tom Crowfoot. 'What the hell did you figure the three of you could do?'

Crowfoot was testing the cinch to his saddle when he replied. 'Why didn't you bring them women with you; as long as it took for you to get here you might as well have brung them along.'

The soldiers were watching the sergeant up ahead with his prisoners and ignored the scouts as they swung astride.

Captain Morris waited until he was sure the prisoners had been disarmed, then turned his back on them and walked his horse toward the scouts. When he got up to them he sat like stone searing each man with a bleak gaze. He did not say a word, just jerked his head and led the way over where the sergeant and his detachment were standing in a circle around their captives.

The sun was slanting away, Al, Tom and Everett borrowed canteens from the soldiers, tanked up, returned the canteens and were as silent as the others around them when they reached the area where the demoralised stockmen were dejectedly standing with their head-hung saddle animals.

As the captain dismounted, and probably without thinking, folded both gauntlets under his belt, the greying cowman whose hair stuck out around his hat, glared and said, 'You blind, mister? Or don't you care that them damned ragheads was trying to catch us to slit our throats?'

Captain Morris looked at each captive individually before speaking. 'Sergeant, tie their hands behind their backs, parcel them out to be led, and let's get back.'

He neither replied to the sullen cowman who had spoken nor looked at him.

# THIRTEEN
## A Deadly Oversight

Because Captain Morris was by nature a taciturn individual, the ride back to the old abandoned ranch buildings was made mostly in silence. Only once did he speak to the scouts; their excuse for leaving the detachment made sense to them, but not to a military officer whose training had instilled in him a conviction that force was only functional when it was unified. People riding off on their own, even when they hadn't actually been ordered not to, seemed almost like a variety of betrayal.

When they reached the buildings there was smoke coming from a chimney. Everett scouted up the place in advance of the column and was waiting with his horse tied in shade when the detachment arrived.

He walked out to tell the captain the two women were inside preparing a meal, then without another word went back where his horses stood, off-saddled the beast, dropped the bridle atop the saddle and bent down to hobble his horse. The animal, wise to hobbles and what they meant, hopped away to find food.

With that example Captain Morris could hardly order the animals tied. He passed word to the sergeant for the animals to be stripped and hobbled, then with the aid of Tom and Al herded his captives to the house, where he was met on the porch by Margaret Halsted, whose face was shiny as she dried both hands on an old towel someone had overlooked when they had abandoned the house.

She gazed at the prisoners. She knew the pair of ranchers but the younger men were strangers to her. She asked the captain who they were and he shrugged. 'I'll find out inside ... Where did you find enough food for the entire detachment, ma'am?'

She coolly considered the officer; they had been like flint on steel since their first meeting. 'The men who were here last night left it, evidently so they could travel light. There won't be enough but it will be adequate until you can get back to my place. There, we'll feed you better. Give us another half hour, Captain.'

He nodded. 'I'll send a couple of men to help,' he said, and turned to call two troopers by name and detail them to help the women. He then drove his prisoners into a large, hot and fragrant kitchen where the Mexican woman watched with round eyes as he and the scouts drove the prisoners through into a large, empty parlour where a massive old stone fireplace, large enough to accommodate half a big log, stood at the north end, and elsewhere other indications that whoever had originally built this place, had thought in terms of size, were evident.

There was nothing to sit on so the captain ordered his prisoners to squat, which they did. So did the scouts, two by the doorless kitchen opening, the other one in front of a closed door leading outside.

The captain was not, initially at any rate, very interested in the identity of his prisoners. His first question was addressed to the wiry, older stockman. 'Where did you get those Gatling guns?'

The cowman, who had anticipated this question, answered in what could have been a truthful manner. 'We bought 'em from a feller named Stebbins couple months back.'

'Who is Stebbins?'

'Darned if we know, Captain.'

The officer gazed at the older man. 'This Stebbins just came along like any other peddler looking for someone who'd buy stolen military hardware, is that it?'

The bulky cowman whose grey hair showed beneath his hat, spoke in a gruff, almost truculent tone of voice. 'I met him, me'n some other fellers, at a saloon in a town at rails end where we drove our cattle. Met him in a saloon an' during a card game we told him damned ragheads had been killin' our cattle and generally raisin' hell an' we was sick an' tired of the army doin' nothing.

'He come right out and offered to sell us Gatling guns and ammunition for 'em. We agreed to buy them.'

'Where did he get them?'

'Damned if I know, Captain, but he had 'em. When our hired freighters went down there, he loaded 'em up an' they started west. If they hadn't stopped for a freighter they picked up along the way hauling supplies at your fort, we'd have got over there without no trouble.' The bushy-headed man glared at Al and Tom. 'Them two come nosin' around.'

The captain already knew about his scouts making an unauthorised sortie. 'What were you going to do with those guns?' he asked, and this time neither cowman replied.

The captain answered for them. 'Go over to Apache Canyon, set up before sunrise, most likely, and as soon as daylight came, start cranking those guns until there was nothing left.'

The cowman and their hired gunmen stared at the floor.

Captain Morris's long silence was only broken when Margaret Halsted appeared in the doorway to inform him a meal was ready. He nodded, left his scouts to watch the prisoners and strode through the kitchen to summon his sergeant to have the troopers file toward the kitchen. He then surprised everyone who saw him do it; he turned back, leaned his saber aside and helped the woman dish out food to hungry soldiers.

The wiry cowman made a close study of the scouts before offering each of them five hundred dollars in gold if they'd open the closed door, and look the other way.

Crowfoot looked at Al Whitten. 'A man can't run far with both hands tied behind his back an' bein' on foot.'

The bulky stockman offered another hundred if they would cut them all loose, and said, 'Don't fret none about horses. There's plenty of 'em out there.'

Al Whitten gazed dispassionately at the burly stockman. 'What's your name, mister?'

'Carl Honig. What's yours?'

'Al Whitten. Mister Honig, you got all that gold on you?'

The wiry man replied. 'No, but we got it an' you'll get it.'

'How? With you gents on the run?'

'We'll cache it for you an' get word back to you where the cache is.'

Al gazed at the wiry man. 'You seriously believe that when you tell some feller to hunt us up an' let us know where the cache is, that he won't raid the cache for himself?'

The wiry man reddened and his burly companion looked sourly at Whitten but said nothing. Not until Everett Tanyard stood in the doorless kitchen opening. What he had to say he stated with obvious disapproval. 'Cap'n says to untie their hands; we're going to feed 'em.'

After Everett turned back into the kitchen Al and Tom gazed at their prisoners for a moment before moving to obey the captain's order. As Tom was untying one of the gunmen, the man looked up and sneered. 'Damn 'breed,' he said.

Tom stepped back with the rope in his hand. Because Al Whitten knew Crowfoot he said, 'Let it go, Tom. Comin' from a son of a bitch like that it's almost a compliment.'

Tom and the sneering gunfighter remained with the burly cowman while Al escorted the other prisoners into the kitchen where they were served a skimpy but hot meal and given water to drink.

Captain Morris stood near the rear door watching them eat, expressionless and silent. Margaret Halsted filled a plate for Al and when he smiled his appreciation, she smiled back. There was a heavy curl of hair hanging over her forehead which she swept away with the back of one hand. 'If we were at the ranch,' she told Whitten, 'I'd feed you better.'

Over the handsome woman's shoulder Al saw the stocky Mexican woman roll her eyes.

There was very little food left. Captain Morris found an empty cup and filled it with water as he watched the prisoners. When they had finished he said, 'Al, be careful,' an admonition Whitten really did not need as he jerked his head for the prisoners to return to the parlour.

'Your turn,' he told Tom Crowfoot, who got to his feet with a gesture for the sneering gunman to precede him. As Al was re-tying the other gunman and his stockmen-employers, the gunfighter spoke almost amiably. 'Name's Hyrum Kaster. Yours is Al Whitten. All me'n Bert Kindig did was hire on to help them cattlemen run off some ragheads. Wasn't a damned thing said about Gatling guns an' the army until we pulled into that burnt village last night.'

Both the burly stockman and the older, wiry man regarded their hired gunfighter dourly.

Al straightened up, his tying completed, and shrugged. 'It's up to the army, Mister Kaster.'

'Not if you'n the 'breed want to pick up a lot of money in gold.'

Al did not even reply, he returned to the place where he had been squatting and wondering how long it was going to be before they left this place. Daylight was still strong, but there was a long ride ahead before they got back over the mountains and down in the direction of the Halsted place.

He thought of the shiny-faced woman in the kitchen. When she smiled it was prettier to see than a summer sunrise. Her companion, Emily Carrera, looked like she'd been raised on quinces. She never smiled, never spoke unless she was either angry or close to it, and the way she had rolled her eyes in the kitchen made Whitten wonder if she didn't disapprove even when Margaret Halsted tried to be friendly.

Tom and his sneering prisoner returned from the kitchen. Al spoke to the man. 'Bert Kindig. I've heard that name somewhere before.'

Tom pointed downward and the gunfighter started to obey when he said, 'Are you a 'breed too?'

Al's reply was non-committal about that. 'We scout for the army. We work as a team. Mister Kindig, did you ever notice when a 'breed an' someone like you cuts a finger, the blood's the same colour?'

Kindig shot a look at his companion, who was listening without much apparent interest. He swung his gaze back to Tom Crowfoot. 'That damned rope was too tight. Not so tight this time.'

Margaret Halsted appeared in the doorway. Behind her the captain said, 'Al, that rider of hers, the feller named Rollie ... He got away last night.'

Before anyone else could speak the sneering gunman laughed, 'One thing soldiers is good at – losin' captives.' He jutted his jaw in the direction of Hyrum Kaster. 'Army had him once. He done better'n than slippin out of his ropes in the dark, he got the lock open on his cell door an' just walked away.'

Every eye turned toward Hyrum Kaster, were still

fixed on him when Bert Kindig spoke again, this time in an altogether different tone of voice; quiet, soft, menacing.

Al's head swung. Kindig was holding a little nickel-plated five-shot revolver in his fist. His hand covered almost half of the small weapon.

Without looking up he said, "Breed, untie these fellers. Cap'n, you be real careful. The first slug'll go through the lady. Real careful. 'Breed, what're you waitin' for; I said cut them ropes loose.'

Tom Crowfoot stared at the little gun, at the face of the man holding it, and looked past Al to Captain Morris, who said, 'Do what he says. Cut them loose.' As Crowfoot drew his knife to obey, the captain addressed the man with the nickel-plated gun. 'Seems the army's pretty poor about goin' over captives for hide-outs.'

Al Whitten's anger seethed, not entirely at the man with the gun, but at the soldiers who had taken the belt-guns from the prisoners without bothering to go over them for belly-guns.

Everett Tanyard came up behind the captain, saw Tom cutting the prisoners free, and soundlessly turned back deeper into the kitchen. No one had noticed him. They were watching Crowfoot as he cut each prisoner free.

Kindig arose, rubbed one wrist with the other one and was about to speak when Captain Morris beat him to it. 'You know how many men are outside around this house? You couldn't get a hundred feet if you had wings.'

The gunmen smiled at the officer. 'I got somethin' better'n wings ... Lady, walk away from him. Walk over here to me.' When Margaret Halsted did not move the gunman cocked his little pistol. '*Walk!*'

She still did not move so the captain gave her a little shove. She crossed the room, which was as silent as a grave, the only sounds coming from outside where men and horses were moving.

Kindig smiled at the officer. 'You saved her life an'

maybe yours too. Now, Captain, come in here away from that doorway. Now go over an' stand by that fireplace. Stand there like you was fixed to the hearth.' After he had been obeyed the gunman gestured toward the box-like holster on Herbert Morris's belt. 'Take the pistol out real careful. Slow. *Slower*! Now then, slide it across the floor toward Hy Kaster.'

Al could have diverted the sliding handgun simply by shoving his leg out. Instead, he let the gun go past. He was trying to estimate his chances of surviving a leaping attack. The gunman was about twelve feet distant, and now his little pistol was cocked. A bolt of lightning could not reach him before he could squeeze the trigger.

He saw Margaret Halsted watching him about the same time the gunman who had seemed so ingratiatingly amiable before, scooped up the captain's handgun as it skittered toward him, and turned toward a shadow he had seen from the corner of his eyes in the kitchen.

Emily Carrera yelped when he caught her in the side with a hard swung pistol barrel. She then turned on him like a tigress calling him every name she could think of in both Spanish and English. The gunman raised his arm without haste and struck her across the face. She collapsed without a sound.

Al, who saw the colour pour into Margaret Halsted's face, spoke quickly. '*Margaret*!' When she turned he shook his head.

Kindig called to his companion in the kitchen. 'Lock that back door … See any soldiers hangin' around out there?'

The sound of the bar being dropped behind the kitchen door was not quite as loud as the voice of the man in the kitchen. 'Naw; some of 'em are nappin' in the shade.'

'Any horses near?'

'Yeah, six or eight. We can't just walk out there and rig up a couple of them, Bert.'

'Sure we can. We got their captain and the woman. Couldn't ask for no better shields, eh Captain?'

Morris still stood in front of the stone fireplace. When he spoke it was to address the stockmen. 'You go with these fools you'll get shot sure as I'm standing here, shields or no shields.'

The wiry man and his friend exchanged a look. The burly man seemed more anxious than the smaller, wiry man. Neither of them made a sound but they both got to their feet and dusted off as Kindig motioned for Margaret Halsted to face the closed front door. As before, she hesitated. Kindig jerked his head in his companion's direction. 'Go shoot the Mex,' he said, then changed it to: 'Go split her skull. No shootin', not yet anyway.'

Margaret did not even look to see if Hyrum Kaster was going into the kitchen. She looked Bert Kindig straight in the eye and nodded. 'I'll go.'

Al Whitten was now farther from the man with the gun as he moved to follow the woman. Kindig's attention was on the woman in front of him and the door. His back was to Whitten. Al eased soundlessly out of a squatting position into a lunging stance for the spring upwards and the catapulting jump.

He did not consider the other gunman, who was over near the kitchen doorway looking in at the unconscious woman with blood trickling across her face from his previous blow. He seemed to be wondering whether there was any reason to strike her again when Tom Crowfoot moved slightly, pulling the gunman's head back around.

After that it was a kaleidoscope of movement. Al Whitten sprang ahead like a ram, head down, arms reaching. Behind him and to his right Tom Crowfoot saw the second gunfighter's arm rising, the gun in the man's hand tracking Whitten as the gunman pulled back the hammer.

Crowfoot hit Hyrum Kaster just below the knees. Force knocked the gunman violently sideward where he struck the wall hard, flexed the finger inside the trigger guard and his gun made a deafening sound in the room as Crowfoot tried to claw his way along the man's body and get a death-grip on his gunwrist.

Before Kaster was struck some instinct warned Bert Kindig of trouble. He spun around, the little nickel-plated gun slicing air for the target he knew was close. What he had a second to see before Whitten's body struck him head on, was a blur with a white face.

Kindig also squeezed the trigger, but not as spasmodically as his companion had done. He fought with considerable strength to bring the gun between himself and the man who rode him to the floor, and almost succeeded when a black boot came in close enough to pin his gun arm to the floor.

With a roar Kindig arched his back and hurled himself sideways. His gun arm came free as Al Whitten rose up enough to aim a drawn-back fist.

Margaret Halsted screamed through the fingers covering her lower face. Whitten felt bone yield as his blow landed, but did not hear the gun when it went off. He heard nothing. The only feeling was as though warm water was trickling somewhere under his clothing.

Captain Morris leaned to wrench away the nickel-plated little revolver and turn where Tom Crowfoot was fighting for his life with the second gunfighter.

The captain turned back as Margaret Halsted dropped to her knees beside Al Whitten. She was unbuttoning his shirt to expose the wound when Captain Morris heard a loud grunt.

Tom Crowfoot was losing his grip on the gun arm of the second gunfighter, who evidently was much stronger than he appeared to be.

Tom was rangy and capable, but this time he was straining until veins stood out on his neck and he was still going to lose his grip.

Captain Morris looked over there again, saw what would happen if the 'breed did not get help, and started toward the doorless kitchen opening when a pistol shot nearly deafened him.

Crowfoot's intense straining nearly sent him sprawling as the man he was fighting did not sag as much as the bullet's force slid him along the floor until his head was against the baseboard. He died staring into Tom Crowfoot's face.

Everett Tanyard eyed the man he had just shot, leaned in the doorway to shuck out the spent casing and shoved the weapon into his waistband. He had shot Hyrum Kaster with the little nickel-plated hideout weapon Bert Kindig had lost in his fight with Al Whitten.

# FOURTEEN
## Desperate Men

Shouting men outside followed the course of the grizzled sergeant and three other men who stormed the house from out back. Other troopers came into the kitchen as the sergeant stopped in the doorless opening where a dead man and a wounded man were lying.

Captain Morris did not raise his head as he told the sergeant to fetch the medical kit and be quick about it.

Everett Tanyard stepped astraddle of the man he had shot and leaned to look closely, as Tom Crowfoot said, 'That's one I owe you. He didn't look as strong as he was.'

Captain Herbert told Margaret Halsted to look after Emily Carrera and the moment she was gone, trailing a bloody skirt, the officer began using a bandana neckerchief to wipe away blood until he saw the little purplish hole where the gunfighter's bullet had hit Whitten.

Tanyard was gazing dispassionately at the man who had shot Whitten, and who was now getting sluggishly to his feet. When the gunman was upright looking around. Everett pulled the gunfighter's little hide-out gun and pointed it. Bert Kindig put both arms out in front as though to ward off a blow.

The crowd of soldiers in the kitchen behind Everett Tanyard were as still and silent as statues. Bert Kindig

144

spoke hoarsely. 'Don't ! It was a fair fight!'

Everett tugged the little trigger, the sound was loud. Bert Kindig turned loose all over and dropped. Captain Morris looked from Kindig to the man in the kitchen doorway who had shot him. Everett was shoving the little gun into his waistband again, looking stonily at the second man he had killed in the old abandoned house. He ignored the officer's stare.

He spoke to Tom Crowfoot in a voice full of disgust. 'That was a damfool thing to do, him with a gun and you on the floor.'

Crowfoot's answer had little to do with the shooting. 'Find some whiskey, Everett. Al's hit hard.'

Tanyard looked at the white faces in the kitchen and one man raised a guarded hand to point in the direction of the sergeant.

Tanyard approached the non-commissioned officer, who was holding Margaret Halsted in his arms. Sobs shook her entire body but she was not making a sound. When Tanyard tapped the sergeant's arm, he got a black glare. Tanyard pulled out the little nickel-plated revolver for the third time and gestured toward the flung-back doorway leading into the yard.

The sergeant, red as a beet, released Margaret Halsted and walked ahead of the scout until they were outside, then he halted and turned, furious and unwilling to take another step until Everett mentioned whiskey and gestured with the little gun.

The sergeant went among staring troopers to the pile of horse equipment which contained his McClellen saddle, dug into one capacious army-issue saddlebag and got back upright holding the bottle. It was two-thirds full. As Everett took it he put up the little gun again and smiled. 'You could lose your stripes, havin' whiskey with you.'

Captain Morris eyed the bottle Everett held out to him and reached for it. Margaret was washing the wounds again. The bleeding had all but stopped. There were two punctures, one slightly below the rib cage where the slug had entered, and another hole in back, up high where it had exited.

As the captain had told the sergeant earlier, it was a good thing those little hide-out pistols used steel jacketed bullets; if that slug had been lead, the exiting wound would have been a jagged hole.

The sergeant had not commented; he had seen more men bleed to death from those big jagged holes than the officer had. He had arisen to hold Margaret Halsted when she appeared to be about to collapse across the unconscious man. Now, standing behind Everett Tanyard, the sergeant watched Margaret Halsted take the bottle from Captain Morris, soak a rag from it and wash the punctures.

The sergeant shook his head. Wounds were washed with water; he'd been risking trouble for the past two months taking that bottle on every detail since he'd bought it at half a month's pay, off a sutler who had passed the fort.

Captain Morris took back the bottle, raised Whitten and got two swallows down the scout. Tom Crowfoot came over to watch, his guess was that the bullet had missed the ribs in front and had come out the back higher and too far to one side to have shattered the shoulder blades, but he would not bet a plugged penny that Al's shoulder bone had not been either nicked or broken.

Tom spoke quietly to the grizzled sergeant. 'Looks like someone's been stickin' hawgs.'

The sergeant turned. 'Go make a travois. Take Everett with you.'

As the pair of 'breeds left the captain looked up at his sergeant. 'How much daylight left?'

'Plenty, sir.' The sergeant pointed. 'Looks like the bleeding's about stopped.'

'Yes, it looks like it has.'

'Well sir, we haul him back over them hills on a travois, an' we might just as well shoot him right here.'

The captain watched Margaret Halsted fashion a massive bandage for Whitten's upper body. He leaned to help her when she tried to balance the unconscious scout with one hand and wrap bandaging with the other hand. Neither of them said a word to the other until Al had been eased down on his back and his eyelids flickered.

She leaned back, watched colour come slowly into the injured man's face, then shot up to her feet and went to care for Emily Carrera. As the officer watched her go, he saw the pair of stockmen. Without a word to either of them he gestured for several onlooking troopers to take them outside. As the soldiers moved to obey, Captain Morris addressed the ranchers. 'I'll put the scouts to watching you directly. Get some idea of getting away if you care to. That dark scout whose name is Everett will be detailed to you.'

He said no more; there actually was nothing more to be said, everyone in the parlour had seen Everett Tanyard kill Bert Kindig.

Al groaned as the cowmen were being taken outside. Tom Crowfoot dropped to one knee. When Whitten's eyes focused Crowfoot was the first person he saw. Whitten made a feeble smile. 'Tom ... What happened?'

Whitten's voice had been low, so Crowfoot leaned down as he replied. 'That son of a bitch got his gun between the pair of you on the floor.'

'How bad is it?'

Instead of replying the scout looked at Captain Morris, who said, 'Bad enough. Unless infection sets in, I'd say you got about a ninety-five per cent chance of recovering. As far as I can determine the slug didn't cause much internal damage, although I'll be damned if I know why it didn't.'

The captain leaned on his heels, his back bothered him every time he remained in a bent over position very long. As he regarded the wounded man he also said, 'You took one hell of a chance.'

Al's gaze was fixed on the officer. 'How's Mrs Halsted?'

The reply came from that doorless opening between the parlour and the kitchen. 'She's fine. So is Emily except for a sore jaw and a cut in the scalp.'

Margaret Halsted walked closer and smiled downward. 'When we get back to the ranch Emily and I'll take care of you.'

Captain Morris stood up, winced from back-pain and regarded Whitten. 'When we get over the mountain, back down into better country, I'll see if the major will detail the post medical officer to look at you. Right now, I don't think you should be moved for a while. You're not bleeding but dragging you back over yonder sure as hell will start it again.'

Whitten closed his eyes. Margaret Halsted put a cool palm on his forehead as the captain cleared his throat and walked out of the house where Everett was sitting with his back to a shed gazing at the two cowmen, neither of whom would look at him.

The captain beckoned to his sergeant. 'Get the men ready,' he said. 'We'll leave as soon as they're saddled up.'

The sergeant glanced at the sun and shrugged. They might be able to get back across the high country before daylight failed, but they would not be able to go farther, unless the captain ordered a night-ride. 'What about the dead men?' he asked. 'If we take time to bury them we'll never get over them mountains before moonrise.'

'Tie them on horses. We'll take them back with us, at least as far as the Halsted place.' As he finished speaking to the sergeant, Captain Morris looked at the pair of cowmen. 'Take a good look around,' he told them. 'My guess is that it'll be years before you see this place again.'

Margaret was in the doorway when the captain started

back. She saw men bringing in horses to be saddled and met the officer with a faint frown. 'You are leaving?'

'Yes'm.'

'But you can't move Mister Whitten.'

'No ma'm. We'll leave him with you.'

'When you pass my ranch will you tell my riders what happened and where we are?'

'If we find any. I'm sorry to leave you like this, but the detail has been gone too long as it is. I'll tell your riders to bring some food over too.'

Margaret went back inside. The captain seemed about to follow her when a burst of fierce profanity came from the direction of the kitchen. He changed his mind and remained outside.

Emily had taken two long pulls off the sergeant's bottle, and while her head still ached and her jaw was slightly swollen, she was on her knees beside Al Whitten when Margaret Halsted approached. Emily looked up. 'What do we do? This one can't be moved.'

Margaret explained that they'd remain where they were, that the soldiers would tell her riders where they were and to bring food, then she stood a long moment looking at Al Whitten without saying a word until Tom Crowfoot came to say he and Everett would stay if she wished, otherwise they would depart with the column.

She thanked him and explained that she and Emily would be all right, that her riders would be along tomorrow some time, and as she watched the 'breed's troubled look at Whitten, she squeezed his hand. 'We'll be all right here. Don't worry. As soon as we can move him we'll take him back to the ranch. You can visit him there.'

Crowfoot left the house and Emily went back to the kitchen to heat water to bathe her torn scalp with. As she did this she kept up a running, one-sided conversation.

'*Soldados*! All over the place – with plenty guns – and you see what happened? And those ranchers – They should have let that dark man take them out a ways and shoot them too. ... *Señora*, this hurt man won't be able to travel for a long time ... Maybe the riders can make a horse-sling. It is much better than those Indian sticks lashed to a horse ... How long do you think we will be here?'

Margaret came to the kitchen doorway, watched Emily putting hot rags atop her head and said, 'For as long as it takes. I don't like the idea of moving him at all, not even in a blanket sling. You can go back if you wish.'

'And leave you here?' Emily rolled her eyes. 'There will be *fantasmas*. Two men died in that room. Their souls will be troubled. I'll stay with you ... *Señora*, I need another swallow from that bottle.'

Margaret got the bottle and watched Emily Carrera take three swallows, not one, then took the bottle back. Al was watching her when she sank down beside him. Outside, there was the sound of mounted men on the move. Tom and Everett came to the doorway to ask again if she did not think they should stay. She shook her head, smiled and thanked them. They departed, but not entirely convinced it was what they should do.

Emily came from the kitchen, holding a wrung out hot cloth to her head, saw Al looking up, and would have shaken her head except that instinct told her not to, so she said, 'Well, *vaquero*, you look better than I feel.' She considered the bulky bandage. 'If we could get you to the ranch ...'

'In a few days, maybe,' Margaret Halsted said. 'But not over the mountain, Emily. We'll take him out by wagon.'

The dark woman's eyes narrowed. 'That old cattle road that goes around the mountains?'

'Yes. I'll have the men go back that way and roll boulders off the roadbed.'

Emily nodded approval. 'The soldiers didn't know about that road?'

'No. And I didn't tell them, they would have wanted to take him back that way on a travois.'

Emily accepted that and shrugged. 'And what about those neighbours of yours they took back with them?'

'That'll be up to the authorities, Emily. I'd guess the military will put them away for many years. One day maybe we can ride to that post and find out.'

'And the Indians, *Señora*?'

Margaret shrugged. Her concern was with the man on the floor. 'See if you can find something to put under him. He'll have to lie here for several days.'

As Emily departed, still holding the rag to her head, Margaret leaned over Al Whitten. 'How do you feel?'

'Weak as a cat.'

She held up the sergeant's bottle until he had swallowed twice then lowered it and arose. 'You need hot food.' She smiled at him. 'Wait right here.'

He smiled back. 'All right, but I had in mind going for a walk.'

The afternoon waned, and with the passing of the sun shadows settled around the old ranch house. Shadows were inside as well, and if they accomplished nothing else they fairly well blanketed the places where blood had dried on the floor.

When the Halsted riders arrived the following day in early afternoon, they were minus one man, Frank Rollie. They had a pack mule with laden *alforas* and they listened stoically as Margaret filled in the areas that Captain Morris had not mentioned.

One of them, a tall, gangling man ugly as original sin with a prominent adam's apple that bobbled when he spoke, examined Al Whitten with experienced hands. When he arose smiling at the scout he said, 'I've seen worse, mister. I was a medical aid man back durin' the war. You'll come out of it, but it'll take time and care.'

Emily Carrera's headache was not quite gone, but unless she moved her head quickly, there was almost no

pain and what there was came from the swollen break in
her scalp which Margaret had bandaged for her,
making her appear ludicrous, something none of the
riders commented on; they knew Emily Carrera's
capacity for invective.

After a large meal the riders prepared to depart.
They would return in a couple of days with a wagon
loaded with straw, but at least one of them, the former
army aid man, had misgivings. As he told Margaret,
maybe Whitten would make it, and maybe he wouldn't.
He hadn't really had enough time for the process of
healing to be very advanced.

She heeded his advice and told them not to return
with the wagon for a week, but to bring more food and
whatever news they acquired within the next day or two.

The last Al Whitten saw of them was when that man
with the bobbing adam's apple came to say they'd be
leaving, and left a small bottle on a windowsill without
explaining to Al what it contained. He admonished Al
against any unnecessary movement, smiled and
departed.

He met Margaret Halsted outside, told her where
he'd left the small bottle and said, 'It's laudanum, ma'm.
If he gets to hurtin' real bad give him a little. Not much,
folks been known to develop a hankering for that stuff.'

Margaret nodded and asked how the rangeman had
happened to have laudanum with him. His reply was
simply stated. 'That captain told us how bad this feller
was hurt. I always keep a little on hand. A person never
knows … Keep him quiet.'

She watched her riders heading south with the sun
getting lower by the moment and wondered if they
would find many large boulders on their way back.

Emily was in hog-heaven; there was enough food to
feed the three of them for weeks. She was preparing a
meal in the kitchen when Margaret took hot coffee to Al
Whitten and cradled his head while he sipped it.

He asked her to tip a little 'Irish' in it, which she did from the sergeant's bottle. As before, his colour improved almost immediately.

Later, as she fed him, he said, 'You should be home runnin' your ranch.'

'In time, Mister Whitten. This is a slack time except for checking drift and watching for first-calf heifers.' She changed the subject. 'You need a shave. I asked my rangeboss to bring my husband's razor over next time.'

Al eyed her askance. 'Ma'm, did you ever use a straight razor?'

She laughed. 'Several times and didn't draw blood.'

'I could maybe shave myself, Mrs Halsted.'

'No. You can't raise either arm as high as your head.' She changed the subject again. 'How long have you scouted for the army?'

'Ten years or so. I'm goin' to quit soon.'

'And then?'

Al looked toward the kitchen doorway where Emily Carrera was watching them. He winked at her; she rolled her eyes skyward as he'd seen her do before and turned back into the kitchen.

'And then, ma'm? I don't rightly know.'

'Mister Whitten, I need another rider to replace the one who was evidently part of the conspiracy to bring in those Gatling guns.'

'Mrs Halsted, I've trailed cattle but haven't ever worked them.'

'But you could. I have a good band of riders, they could teach you.'

He eyed her quizzically. 'You could hire another rider. This time of year they're lookin' for work.'

'I'm not hard to work for, Mister Whitten,' she told him, returning his dead-level gaze, and showed a little feminine guile when she said, 'I'd appreciate it. It's not easy for a woman to run a cow outfit. I need all the help I can get.'

He heard a snort in the vicinity of the kitchen and ignored it. 'Well, there's somethin' else, Mrs Halsted ... It'd be hard for me to work for you.'

'Why?'

'Well; for one thing you're more woman than I've seen in a lot of years, and that'd make it hard for me; learnin' an' thinkin' of you at the same time.'

She laughed softly at him. 'Would it be any easier if I called you Al and you called me Margaret?'

He sighed. 'It would make it harder.'

'Please try, Al.'

He drifted his gaze from her to the doorless kitchen opening. Emily Carrera was standing there again, drying her hands on a ragged cloth. She looked straight back and nodded her head.

He said, 'I'll try ... Margaret.'

She left him to see where their horses were, and during her absence Emily Carrera came forward to adjust his pallet and looked him squarely in the eye as she said, '*Señor*, for a man your age you are as thick as oak.'

He looked into the dark, round face. 'I did somethin' wrong?'

Emily sat back on her heels balancing a candid reply in her mind, then, instead of answering shrugged her shoulders and stood up. From over in the doorless kitchen opening she said, 'She is a handsome woman.'

Al agreed. 'Very handsome.'

'And very lonely for a long time.'

Al watched the woman moving around in the kitchen until he fell asleep.

Four days later, when the women had cobbled together a better bed for him and Emily had given him a bath, Tom Crowfoot rode into the yard accompanied by Captain Morris. They gazed at the wounded man, exchanged a look and the officer put a bottle of tequila beside Whitten's pallet without saying a word until

Margaret appeared, then he told her why he and Tom Crowfoot had ridden so far.

'The In'ians left Apache Canyon. Tom and I scouted it up; not an In'ian anywhere around, many tracks of a large band heading south.'

Crowfoot told Al Whitten he thought it probable that after those Indians they had encountered in the dark, brushy arroyo got back to their rancheria in the canyon, they had palavered. It was Tom's opinion that the wise heads among them had decided that if someone had come close to causing a massacre with Gatling guns above their canyon, their age-old home ground would continue to be vulnerable, and Tom thought that wide trail leading south from Apache Canyon was the inhabitants of their ancestral home abandoning the canyon. Tom smiled wolfishly. 'South they went lock stock and barrel. They'll find another place to set up an' my guess is that it'll be much closer to the Mex border. They raid down into Messico with greater success than they do up here.

'Up here, it's gettin' too crowded with ranchers, settlers an' soldiers. They didn't have to be real smart to figure out how close they come to gettin' wiped out this time.'

Emily fed the visitors and asked where the very dark scout named Tanyard was. Tom Crowfoot replied with a perfectly straight face. 'Ma'm, he wouldn't come with us because he was scairt you'd want to marry him.'

Emily's face showed nothing for seconds, then showed dark colour as she exploded. Captain Morris's ears burned but he acted as though he were deaf. Not until the tirade ended and he looked at Margaret Halsted did he offer a comment. 'Fine weather we've been having.'

Al saw Margaret struggling to keep from laughing as she replied. 'Very nice weather indeed, Captain, but we need rain.'

When the women were in the kitchen after the meal

Tom hunkered down beside Al and said, 'You remember that freighter who hauled us in his wagon?'

'Curtis Glidden? What about him?'

'As the column passed through what was left of Burnt Timbers some hard nosed townsmen had impounded his hitch. The wagon got burnt but his horses was unharmed. Cap'n told them fellers to hand over his team.'

'Did they do it?'

'They done it. I told the freighter what had happened an' that you got shot. He said for me to tell you he wished you to get better. Last I saw, he was ridin' one horse an' leadin' the other one.'

'What did the captain do with his prisoners?'

'We rounded up five more, took 'em all back to the fort an' they're in the guardhouse until a military court can be set up. Al, I heard the major tell the cap'n he wished he had authority to hang 'em.'

Tom leaned closer. 'When'll you be able to come back?'

'Never. Well, long enough to get my gatherings, then I'm goin' to become a rangeman.'

Crowfoot's eyes got round. 'You, a rangeman. You never …'

'Mrs Halsted's riders will teach me.'

'You're going to work for a woman?'

Al smiled slightly. 'You ever see a prettier one, Tom?'

'No, but that's got nothin' to do with workin' for one. They tell me women are awful hard to work for; they're cranky and fidgety an' –'

'I told you I was goin' to quit working for the army.'

'Yes, but … You could get a job in town, maybe with the blacksmith, maybe as a barman –'

'What town?'

'Any town,' Crowfoot said, and got upright as the captain and Margaret Halsted entered the room. The captain was his cryptic self. 'We should start back, Tom.'

Crowfoot left the house to rig their horses. Captain Morris leaned to shake Whitten's hand, straightened up, nodded gallantly toward Margaret Halsted, and went outside.

Emily, busy in the kitchen, came to the parlour with a fierce look. 'Me, marry that In'ian! I thought he was crazy when he pulled me off my horse. Now I know he was crazy,' she exclaimed.

Margaret lingered in the parlour. 'Al ...?'

'Yes'm?'

They both heard the loud snort from the kitchen, and Margaret said, 'We'll talk later.'